The Scotch Twins

Lucy Fitch Perkins

THE SCOTCH TWINS

I. THE LITTLE GRAY HOUSE ON THE BRAE

If you had peeped in at the window of a little gray house on a heathery hillside in the Highlands of Scotland one Saturday morning in May some years ago, you might have seen Jean Campbell "redding up" her kitchen. It was a sight best seen from a safe distance, for, though Jean was only twelve years old, she was a fierce little housekeeper every day in the week, and on Saturday, when she was getting ready for the Sabbath, it was a bold person indeed who would venture to put himself in the path of her broom. To be sure, there was no one in the family to take such a risk except her twin brother Jock, her father, Robin Campbell, the Shepherd of Glen Easig, and True Tammas, the dog, for the Twins' mother had "slippit awa'" when they were only ten years old, leaving Jean to take a woman's care of her father and brother and the little gray house on the brae.

On this May morning Jean woke up at five o'clock and peeped out of the closet bed in which she slept to take a look at the day. The sun had already risen over the rocky crest of gray old Ben Vane, the mountain back of the house, and was pouring a stream of golden sunlight through the eastern windows of the kitchen. The kettle was singing over the fire in the open fireplace, a pan of skimmed milk for the calf was warming by the hearth, and her father was just going out, with the pail on his arm, to milk the cow. She looked across the room at the bed in the corner by the fireplace to see if Jock were still asleep. All she could see of him was a shock of sandy hair, two eyes tight shut, and a freckled nose half buried in the bed-clothes.

"Wake up, you lazy laddie," she called out to him, "or when I get my clothes on I'll waken you with a wet cloth! Here's the sun looking in at the windows to shame you, and Father already gone to the milking."

Jock opened one sleepy blue eye.

"Leave us alone, now, Jeanie," he wheedled. "I was just having a sonsie wee bit of a dream. Let me finish, and syne I'll tell you all about it."

"Indeed, and you'll do nothing of the kind" retorted Jean, with spirit. "Up with you, mannie, or I'll be dressed before you, and I ken very well you'd not like to be beaten by a lassie, and her your own sister, too."

Jock cuddled down farther into the blankets without answering, and Jean began putting on her clothes. It seemed but a moment before she slid to the floor, rolled her sleeves high above a pair of sturdy elbows, and went to finish her toilet at the basin. There she washed her face and combed her hair, while Jock, cautiously opening one eye again, observed her from his safe retreat. He watched her part her hair, wet it, plaster it severely back from her brow, and tie it firmly in place with a piece of black ribbon. Jock could read Jean's face like print, and in this stern toilet he foresaw a day of unrelenting house-cleaning.

"Aye," he said to himself bitterly, "she's putting on her Saturday face. There's trouble brewing, I doubt! It'll be Jock this and Jock that both but and ben all day long, and whatever is the use of all this tirley-wirly I can't see, when on Monday the house will look as if it had never seen the sight of a besom! I'll just bide where I am." He closed his eyes and pretended to be asleep.

It is true that Jean's Saturday face had such a housekeepery pucker between the eyes and such a severe arrangement of the front hair that any one who did not peep behind the black ribbon might have thought her a very stern young person indeed, but behind the black ribbon Jean's true character stood revealed! However prim and smooth she might make it look in front, where the cracked glass enabled her to keep an eye on it, behind her back, where she couldn't possibly see it, her hair broke into the jolliest little waves and curls, which bobbed merrily about even on the worst Saturday that ever was; and spoiled the effect whenever she tried to be severe.

When she had given a final wipe with the brush, she took another look at Jock. There was still nothing to be seen of him but the shock of sandy hair and a series of bumps under the blanket. Jock could feel Jean looking at him right through the bed-clothes.

"Jock," said Jean,—and her voice had a Saturday sound to it,—"You can't sleep in this day! Get up!"

There was no answer. Jock might well have known that Jean was in no mood for trifling, but, having decided on his course of action, he stuck to it like a true Scotchman and neither moved nor opened his eyes. Jean was driven to desperate measures. She took a few drops of water in the dipper, marched firmly to the bedside, and stood with it poised directly above Jock's nose.

"Jock," she said solemnly, "I'm telling you! Don't ever say I didn't. If you don't stir yourself before I count five, you'll be sorry. One, two, three!" Still no move from Jock. "Four, five," and, without further parley, she emptied the dipper on his freckled nose.

There was a wrathful snort and a violent convulsion of the blankets, and an instant later Jock was tearing about the kitchen like a cat in a fit, but by this time Jean was out of doors and well beyond reach.

"Come here, you limmer!" he howled. But Jean knew better than to accept his invitation. Instead she skipped laughing down the path from the door to the brook which ran bubbling and gurgling by the house. Even in her hasty exit from the cottage, Jean had had the presence of mind to take the pail with her, and now she stopped to fill it from the clear, sparkling water of the burn. It was such a wonderful bright spring morning that, having filled it, she stopped for a moment to look about her at the dear familiar surroundings of her home.

There was the little gray house itself, with the peat smoke curling from the chimney straight up into the blue sky. Back of it was the garden-patch with its low stone wall, and back of that were the fowl-yard and the straw-covered byre for the cow. Beyond, and to the north lay the moors, covered with heather and dotted with grazing sheep. Jean could hear the tinkle of their bells, the bleating of the lambs, and the comforting maternal answers of the ewes. Above the dark forest which spread itself over the slopes of the foot-hills toward the south and east a lave rock was singing, and she could hear the cry of whaups wheeling and circling over the moors. They were pleasant morning sounds, dear and familiar to Jean's ear, and oh, the sparkle of the dew on the bracken, and the smell of the hawthorn by the garden wall! Jean lifted her pail of water and went singing with it up the hill-slope to the house for sheer joy that she was alive.

"The Campbells are coming, O ho, O ho!" she sang, and the hills, taking up the refrain, echoed "O ho, O ho!"

True Tammas, who had slept all night under the straw-stack by the byre, came bounding down the little path to meet her, wagging his tail and barking his morning greeting. They reached the door together, but Jock, mindful of his injuries, had shut and barred it, and was grinning at them through the window. Jean sat placidly down upon the step with True Tammas beside her and continued her song. Her calmness irritated Jock.

"Aye," he shouted through the crack, "the Campbells may be coming, but they'll not get in this house! You can just sit there blethering all day, and I'll never unbar the door."

Jean stopped singing long enough to answer: "You'll get no breakfast, then, you mind, unless you'll be getting it yourself, for the porridge is not cooked and the kettle's nearly boiled away. I've the water-pail with me, and there's not a drop else in the house."

She left him to consider this and resumed her song. For several minutes she and True Tammas sat there gazing westward across the valley with the little river flowing through it, to the hills swimming in the blue distance beyond.

At last she called over her shoulder, "Jock, Father's coming," and Jock, seeing that his cause was hopelessly lost, unfastened the door. Jean, her father, and True Tammas all came into the kitchen together, and the moment she was in the room again you should have seen how she ordered things about!

"Set the milk right down here, Father," she said, tapping the table with her finger as she flew past to get the strainer and a pan, "and you, Jock, fill the kettle. It's almost dry this minute. And stir up the fire under it. Tam," — that was what they called the dog for short,—"go under the table or you'll get stepped on!"

You should have seen how they all minded!—even the father, who was six feet tall, with a jaw like a nut-cracker and a face that would have looked very stern indeed if it hadn't been for his twinkling blue eyes. When the milk was strained and put away in the little shed room back of the kitchen chimney, Jean got out the oatmeal-kettle and hung the porridge over the fire, and while that was cooking she set three places at the tiny table and scalded the churn. Meanwhile Jock went out to feed the fowls. By half past six the oatmeal was on the table and the little family gathered about it, reverently bowing their heads while the Shepherd of Glen Easig asked a blessing upon the food.

There was only porridge and milk for breakfast, so it took but a short time to eat it, and then the real work of the day began. The Shepherd put on his Kilmarnock bonnet and called Tam, who had had his breakfast on the hearth, and the two went away to the hills after the sheep. Jock led the cow to a patch of green turf near the bottom of the hill, where she could find fresh pasture, and Jean was left alone in the kitchen of the little gray house. Ah, you should have seen her then! She washed the dishes and put them away in the cupboard, she skimmed the milk and put the cream into the churn, she swept the hearth and shook the blankets out of doors in the fresh morning air. Then she made the beds, and when the kitchen was all in order, she "went ben"—that was the way they spoke of the best room— and dusted that too. There wasn't really a bit of need of dusting the room, for it was never, never used except on very important occasions, such as when the minister called. The little house was five miles from the village, so the minister did not come often, but Jean kept it clean all the time just to be on the safe side.

There wasn't so very much work to do in the room after all, for there was nothing in it but the fireplace, a little table with the Bible, the Catechism, and a copy of Burns's poems on it, and three chairs. The kitchen was a different matter: There were the beds, and they were hard for a small girl to manage, and the cupboard with its shelves of dishes. There were three stools, and a big chair for the Shepherd, and the great chest where the clothes were kept, and besides all these things there was the wag-at-the-wall clock on the mantel-shelf which had to be wound every Saturday night. If you want to know just where these things stood, you have only to look at the plan, where their places are so plainly marked that, if you were suddenly to wake up in the middle of the night and find yourself in the little gray house, you could go about and put your hand on everything in it in the dark.

Jock stayed with the cow as long as he dared, and went back to the house only when he knew he couldn't postpone his tasks any longer. Jean was sweeping the doorstep as he came slowly up the hill.

"Come along, Grandfather," she called out, her brow sternly puckered in front and her curls bobbing gaily up and down behind. "A body'd think you were seventy-five years old and had the rheumatism to see you move! Come and work the churn a bit. 'Twill limber you up."

Jock knew that arguments were useless. His father had told him, girl's work or not, he was to help Jean, so he slowly dragged into the house and slowly began to move the dasher up and down.

"Havers!" said Jean, when she could stand it no longer. "It's lucky there's a cover to the churn else you'd drop to sleep and fall in and drown yourself in the buttermilk! The butter won't be here at this rate till to-morrow, when it would break the Sabbath by coming!"

She seized the dasher, as she spoke, and began to churn so vigorously that the milk splashed up all around the handle. Soon little yellow specks began to appear; and when they had formed themselves into a ball in the churn, she lifted it out with a paddle and put it in a pan of clear cold water. Then she gave Jock a drink of buttermilk.

"Poor laddie!" she said. "You are all tired out! Take a sup of this to put new strength in you, for you've got to go out and weed the garden. I looked at the potatoes yesterday, and the weeds have got the start of them already."

"If I must weed the garden, give me something to eat too," begged Jock. "This milk'll do no more than slop around in my insides to make me feel my emptiness."

Jean opened the cupboard door and peeped within.

"There's nothing for you, laddie," she said, "but this piece of a scone. I'll have to bake more for the Sabbath, and you can have this to give yourself a more filled-up feeling. And now off with you!"

She took him by the collar and led him to the door; and there on the step was Tam.

"What are you doing here?" cried Jean, astonished to see him. "You should be with Father, watching the sheep! It's shame to a dog to be lolling around the house instead of away on the hills where he belongs."

Tam flattened himself out on his stomach and dragged himself to her feet, rolling his eyes beseechingly upward, and if ever a dog looked ashamed of himself, that dog was Tam. Jean shook her head at him very sternly, and oh, how the jolly little curls bobbed about.

"Tam," she said, "you're as lazy as Jock himself. Whatever shall I do with the two of you?"

Jock had already finished his scone and he thought this a good time to disappear. He slipped round the corner of the house and whistled. All Tam's shame was gone in an instant. He gave a joyous bark and bounded away after Jock, his tail waving gayly in the breeze.

II. THE RABBIT AND THE GAMEKEEPER

Out in the garden a rabbit had for some time been enjoying himself nightly in the potato-patch, biting off the young sprouts which were just sticking their heads through the ground. When the rabbit heard Tam bark she dashed out of sight behind a burdock leaf and sat perfectly still. Now if Tam and Jock had come into the garden by the wicket gate, as they should have done, this story might never have been written at all, because in that case the rabbit would perhaps have got safely back to her burrow in the woods without being seen, and there wouldn't have been any story to tell.

But Tam and Jock didn't come in by the gate. They jumped over the wall. Jock jumped first and landed almost on top of the rabbit, but when Tam, a second later, landed in the same place, she was running for dear life toward the hole in the stone wall where she had got in. Shouting and barking, Jock and Tam tore after her. Round and round the garden they flew, but just as they thought they had her cornered, the rabbit slipped through the hole in the wall and ran like the wind for the woods. Jock and Tam both cleared the wall at a bound and chased after her, making enough noise to be heard a mile away.

It happened that there was some one much less than a mile away to hear it. And it happened, too, that he was the one person in all the world that Jock would most wish not to hear it, for he was gamekeeper to the Laird of Glen Cairn, and the Laird of Glen Cairn owned all the land for miles and miles about in every direction. He owned the little gray house and the moor, the mountain, and the forest, and even the little brook that sang by the door. To be sure, the Laird seemed to care very little for his Highland home. He visited it but once in a great while, and then only for a few days' hunting. The rest of the year his great stone castle was occupied only by Eppie McLean, the housekeeper, and two or three other servants. The Laird did not know his tenants, and they did not know him. The rents were collected for him by Mr. Craigie, his factor, who lived in the village, and Angus Niel was appointed to see that no one hunted game on the estate.

Angus was a man of great zeal in the performance of his duty, to judge by his own account of it. He was always telling of heroic encounters with poachers in the forests, and though he never seemed to succeed in catching them and bringing them before the magistrate, his tales were a warning to evil-doers and few people dared venture into the region which he guarded. He was often seen creeping along the outskirts of the woods, his gun on his shoulder, his round eyes rolling suspiciously in every direction, or even loitering around the cow byres as if he thought game might be secreted there.

At the very moment when Jock and Tam came flying over the fence and down the hill like a cyclone after the rabbit, Angus was kneeling beside the brook to get a drink. His lips were pursed up and he was bending over almost to the surface of the water, when something dashed past him, and an instant later something else struck him like a thunderbolt from behind, and drove him headforemost into the brook! It wasn't Tam that did it. It was Jock! Of course, it was an accident, but Angus thought he had done it on purpose, and he was probably the most surprised as well as the angriest man in Scotland at that moment. He lifted his head out of the brook and glared at Jock as fiercely as he could with little rills of water pouring from his hair and nose, and trickling in streams down his neck.

"I'll make you smart for this, you young blatherskite," he roared at Jock, who stood before him frozen with horror. "I'll teach you where you belong! You were running after that rabbit, and your dog is yelping down a hole after her this minute!" He was such a funny sight as he knelt there, dripping and scolding, that, scared as he was, Jock could not help laughing. More than ever enraged, Angus made a sudden lunge forward and seized Jock by the ear.

"You come along o' me," he said. His invitation was so urgent that Jock felt obliged to accept it, and together the two started up the slope to the little gray house. Tam, meanwhile, had given up the chase and joined them, his tail at half-mast.

When they reached the house Angus bumped the door open without knocking, and stamped into the kitchen. Jean was bending over the fire turning a scone on the girdle, when the noise at the door made her jump and look around. She was so amazed at the sight which met her eye that for an instant she stood stock-still, and Angus, seeing that he had only two children to deal with, gave Jock's ear a vicious tweak and began to bluster at Jean.

But, you see, he didn't know Jean. When she saw that great fat man abusing her brother and tracking mud all over her kitchen floor at the same time, instead of being frightened, as she should have been, Jean shook her cooking-fork at Angus Niel and stamped her foot smartly on the floor.

"You let go of my brother's ear this instant," she shouted, "and take your muddy boots out of my kitchen!"

Angus let go of Jock's ear for sheer surprise, and Jock at once sprang to his sister's side, while Tam, seeing that trouble was brewing, gave a low growl and bared his teeth. Angus gave a look at Tam and decided to explain.

"This young blatherskite here," he began, in a voice that caused the rafters to shake, "has been trespassing. He was after a rabbit. I caught him in the very act. I'll have the law on him! He rammed me into the burn!"

"I didn't mean to," shouted Jock, "I thought you were a stone, and I just meant to step on you and jump across the burn."

"You meant to step on me, did you?" roared Angus. "Me! Do you know who I am?" Jock knew very well, but he didn't have time to say so before Angus, choking with rage, made a furious lunge for his ear and left two more great spots of mud on the kitchen floor. It was not to be borne. Jean pointed to his feet.

"You're trespassing yourself," she screamed. "You've no right in this house, And you take yourself out of it this minute! Just look at the mud you've tracked on my floor!"

Angus did look. He looked not only at the floor but at Tam, for Tam was now slowly approaching him, growling as he came.

Angus thought best to do exactly as Jean said and as quickly as possible. He reached the door in two jumps with Tam leaping after him and nipping his heels at each jump, and in another instant found himself on the doorstep with the door shut behind him.

Angus considered himself a very important man. He wasn't used to being treated in this way, and it's no wonder he was angry. He swelled up like a pouter pigeon; and shook his fist at the door.

"You just mind who I am," he shouted. "If ever I catch you poaching again, I'll have you up before the bailie as sure as eggs is eggs!"

But the door didn't say a word, and it seemed beneath his dignity to scold a door that wouldn't even answer back, so he stamped away growling. The children watched him until he disappeared in the woods, and when at last they turned from the window, the scone on the girdle was burned to a cinder and had to be given to the chickens!

You might have thought that by this time Jean had done enough work even for Saturday, but there was still the broth to make for supper and for the Sabbath, and the kitchen floor to be scrubbed, and, last of all, the family baths! When the little kitchen was as clean as clean could be, Jean got the wash-tub and set it on the hearth. Jock knew the signs and decided he'd go out behind the byre and look for eggs, but Jean had her eye on him.

"Jock Campbell," said she, "you go at once and get the water."

In vain Jock assured her he was cleaner than anything and didn't need a bath. Jean was firm. She made him fill the kettles, and when the water was hot, she shut him up in the kitchen with soap and a towel while she took all the shoes to the front steps to polish for Kirk on the morrow. When at last Jock appeared before her he was so shiny clean that Jean said it dazzled her eyes to look at him, so she sent him for the cow while she took her turn at the tub.

By four o'clock, Tam, who had spent an anxious afternoon by the hole in the garden wall watching for the rabbit, suddenly remembered his duties and started away over the moors to meet the Shepherd and round up any sheep that might have strayed from the flock, and at five Jock, returning from the byre, met his father coming home with Tam at his heels.

The regular evening tasks were finished just as the sun sank out of sight behind the western hills, and the birds were singing their evening songs, and when they went into the kitchen a bright fire was blazing on the hearth, the broth was simmering in the kettle, and Jean had three bowls of it ready for them on the table.

While they ate their supper Jock told their father all about the rabbit and Angus Niel and his ducking in the burn, and when Jock told about Jean's ordering him out of the kitchen, and of his jumping to the door with Tam nipping at his heels, the Shepherd slapped his knee and laughed till he cried. Tam, sitting on the hearth with his tongue lolling out, looked as if he were laughing, too.

"Havers!" cried the Shepherd, "I wish I'd been here to see that sight! Angus is that swollen up with pride of position, he's like to burst himself. He needed a bit of a fall to ease him of it, but I'd never have picked out Jean Campbell to trip him up! You're a spirited tid, my dawtie, and I'm proud of you."

"But, Father," said Jock, "whatever shall we do about the rabbits? The woods are full of them, and there'll not be a sprig of green left in the garden. They can hop right over the wall, even if we do stop up the hole."

"Aye," answered his father solemnly, "and that's a serious question, my lad. They get worse every year, and syne we'll have no tatties for the winter, let alone other vegetables. A deer came into Andrew Crumpet's garden one night last week and left not a green sprout in it by the morning. The creatures must live that idle gentlemen may shoot them for pleasure, even though they eat our food and leave us to go hungry." His brow darkened and a long-smouldering wrath burst forth into words. "There's no justice in it," he declared, thumping the table with his fist till the spoons danced, "Lairds or no Lairds, Anguses or no Anguses."

The Twins had never before heard their father speak like that, and they were a little frightened. They were too young to know the long years of injustice in such matters that stretched far back into the history of Scotland.

For a few minutes after this outburst the Shepherd remained silent, gazing into the fire; then he roused himself from his brown study and said: "I've been keeping something from you, my bairns. Mr. Craigie told me last week that the Auld Laird has taken a whim to turn all this region into a game preserve, and that he will not renew our lease when the time is up. It has till autumn to run, and then, God help us, we'll have to be turned out of this house where I've lived all my life and my forebears before me, and seek some other place to live and some other work to do."

"But what can you do else?" gasped Jock. He felt that his world was tumbling about his ears.

"The Lord knows," answered the Shepherd. "Emigrate to America likely. I've always been with the sheep and nothing else. It may be I can hire out to some other body, but chances are few hereabouts, and if the Auld Laird carries out this notion, there'll be many another beside ourselves who'll need to be walking the world. It seems unlikely he would be for taking away the town too, even if it is but a wee bit of a village, and the law gives him the right, for times have changed since that lease was made, long years ago, and there are few in this day who would venture to enforce it. But the Auld Laird's a hard man, I'm told, and he chooses hard men to carry out his will. Mr. Craigie has little heart, and as for Angus Niel, he'd make things worse rather than better if he had his way." Then, seeing tears gathering in Jean's eyes, he said to comfort her, "There now, dinna greet, my lassie! There's no sense in crossing a bridge till you come to it, and this bridge is still four months and a bittock away. We've the summer before us, and the Lord's arm is not shortened that it cannot save. We'll make the best of it and have one more happy summer, let the worst come at the end of it."

"But, Father," urged Jock, "will he turn every one out, do you think?"

"Who can foretell the whimsies of a selfish man?" answered the Shepherd. "He has only his own will to consider, but my opinion is he'll turn out those whose holdings lie nearest the forests and would be best for game, whatever he may do with the rest."

This was overwhelming news, and the children sat silent beside their silent father, trying to think of something to comfort their sad hearts. At last Jean lifted her head with a spirited toss and said, "Gin we were to go to-morrow, the dishes would still have to be washed," and she began to clear the table.

Her father laughed, and oh, how his laugh brightened the little kitchen and seemed to bid defiance to the fates!

"That's right, little woman," he said. "You've the true spirit of a Campbell in you. We must aye do the duty at hand and trust the Lord for the rest."

Jock was so impressed with the solemn talk of the evening that he wiped the dishes without being asked and went to bed of his own accord when the wag-at-the-wall clock struck eight. The Shepherd sat alone beside the fire until the children were in bed and asleep; then he sent Tam to the straw stack, wound the clock, and took his own turn at the tub. Last of all he covered the coals with ashes for the night and crept into bed beside Jock.

III. THE SABBATH

The Sabbath morning dawned bright and clear, and the Campbells were all up early and had the chores done before seven o'clock. Then came breakfast, and after breakfast Jean ran "ben the room," and brought the Bible to her father. Then she and Jock sat with folded hands while he read a long chapter about the "begats." Jock thought there seemed to be a very large family of them. This was followed by a prayer as long as the chapter. The prayer was so long that True Tammas went sound asleep on the hearth and had a dream that must have been about the rabbit, for his ears twitched and he made little whiny noises and jerked his legs. It was so long that the kettle boiled clear away and made such alarming, crackling sounds that Jean couldn't help peeking through her fingers just once, because it was their only kettle, and if it should go and burst itself during family prayers, whatever should they do! The moment the Shepherd said "Amen," Jean sprang so quickly to lift it from the fire that she stumbled over Tam and woke him up and almost burned her fingers besides. The kettle wasn't really spoiled, and while the water was heating in it for the dishes, Jean took up the little yellow book and said to Jock,

"Come here now, laddie, and see if you can say your catechism. Do you ken what is the chief end of man?"

"Dod, and I do," answered Jock. "You let me spier the questions."

"No," answered Jean firmly. "I'll spier them first myself."

"You're thinking I can't answer," said Jock. "I'll fool you."

He stood up as straight as a whole row of soldiers and fired off the answer all in one breath.

"The-chief-end-of-man-is-to-glorify-God-and-enjoy-Him-forever," he shouted.

Jean nodded approvingly. "You ken that one all right, but that is the first one in the book and everybody knows that one. Now I'm going to skip around."

"Don't skip," urged Jock. "Take them just the way they come. I can remember 'em better."

But Jean gave no quarter. "What is predestination?" she demanded.

This was a poser, but Jock tackled it bravely.

"Whom he did foreknow he also did predestinate to-to-" he got so far and stuck.

"To what?" asked Jean.

"To be reformed," Jock hazarded, wallowing in difficulties.

"Conformed," corrected Jean. "You don't know that one at all! What is Saving Grace?"

Jock fell down entirely on saving grace. "It's a—It's a—" he began. Then he bit his lip and scowled, and looked up at the ham hanging from the rafters, and out of the windows, but as nothing more about saving grace occurred to him he said, "Aw, Jean, I know, but I can't think."

"If you knew, you wouldn't have to think," Jean retorted, and then she made him take the book and sit down on the stool by the window and learn both answers while she finished the dishes.

It was ten miles to the village and back, and there was no way to get there except by walking, but the Campbells would sooner have thought of going without their food than of staying away from the Kirk, and so by eight o'clock they were all dressed in their best clothes and ready to start. They left True Tammas sitting on the doorstep with his ears drooped and his eyes looking very sorrowful. He wanted to go with them, but he knew well that he must stay at home to guard the sheep from stray dogs.

It was springtime, and the world was so lovely that the troubles the little family had faced the evening before seemed far away and impossible in the morning light. It was as if they had awakened from a bad dream. Who could help being happy on such a morning? The birds were flying about with straw and bits of wool in their bills to weave into their nests, and singing as if they would split their little throats. The river splashed and gurgled and sang as it dashed over its rocky bed on its way to the sea.

From the village came the distant music of the church bells. The hawthorn was in bloom, and the river-banks and roadsides were gay with dandelions and violets, daisies and buttercups. Far away the mountains lifted their blue summits to the sky, and on a nearer hill they could see the gray towers of the castle of the Laird of Glen Cairn.

The bell was ringing its final summons and all the people were pouring into the little vestibule as the Campbells reached the steps of the Kirk. Angus Niel pushed past them, looking as puffy as a turkey-cock with its feathers spread, and glaring at the Twins so fiercely that Jock whispered to Jean, "If I poked my finger at him I believe he'd gobble," and made her almost laugh aloud. When they passed Mr. Craigie, who held the plate for people to drop their money in, Jean whispered to Jock, "He looks for all the world like a pair of tongs in his blacks, he's that tall and thin," and then Jock certainly would have laughed outright if he hadn't seen Mrs. Crumpet's eye on him.

The sermon was very long and the seats were hard and high, but the service did come to an end at last, although Jock was sure it was never going to, and afterward the children with their father stood about in the churchyard for a little while talking to their neighbors and friends.

The farm of Andrew Crumpet lay in the same direction as the home of the Campbells, so it was natural that they should walk along together and that the two men should talk about the thing that was uppermost in their minds. Mrs. Crumpet had gone on ahead with another neighbor, and Sandy Crumpet, who was twelve too, and had yellow hair, a snub nose, and freckles like Jock's own, walked with the Twins behind the two fathers. As they turned into the road, the children heard Andrew say, with a heavy sigh: "Aye, Robin, we must just make up our minds to it. The Auld Laird's bent on getting us out."

"Has Mr. Craigie given you notice, too?" asked the Shepherd.

"Aye, has he," Andrew answered with bitterness, "and short work he made of it. It means little to him telling a man to leave his home and go out in the world to seek new work at our time of life."

"He passes for a religious man," said the Shepherd.

"So did the Pharisee in the temple," said Andrew, "but 'by their fruits ye shall know them,' and we're not gathering any figs off of Mr. Craigie, nor grapes from that thorn of an Auld Laird that I can see!"

"Nor from Angus Niel, either," agreed Robin Campbell. "The Auld Laird's servants are of a piece with himself."

"Fine I ken that," answered Andrew.

"Well," sighed the Shepherd, "the toad under the harrow cannot be expected to praise the plowman, and we're just like the toad."

"Very true," said Andrew, "but the toad has the best of it. We are being destroyed; not that some one may till the land, but that it may go to waste, and be kept out of use. We suffer that the rich may be richer and the poor poorer, that less food may be produced instead of more. I tell you, Robin, it is not justice."

"It may be so. It may be so," sighed the Shepherd, "but it is the law, and we must just submit."

The two men walked on in silence to the bridge, where the Crumpets turned, while the Campbells kept on beside the river. The children were silent, too, only calling out "Good-bye" to Sandy as they parted, Jock adding, "Come on by to-morrow if you can," and Sandy, waving his hand, calling back, "Aye, will I."

As the Twins and their father neared the "wee bit hoosie," Tam came bounding down the brae to meet them, and in less time than it takes to tell it Jean had run into the house, taken off her Sabbath dress, and put on her old one, with her kitchen apron over it, had mended the fire and heated the broth, and the little family was seated about the table eating their frugal meal with appetites sharpened by their long walk.

The afternoon seemed endless to the children, for they spent it trying hard not to do any of the things they wanted to do. They studied the catechism while their father sat with his bonnet on his head nodding over the Bible, and the wag-at-the-wall clock ticked the hours solemnly away. Jock whispered to Jean that he didn't see why Sunday was so much longer than any other day, and didn't believe her when she said it wasn't really that it only seemed so.

IV. THE NEW BOY

Usually Jean and Jock went to school in summer, for in winter the snow made the roads impassable, but at this time the Dominie was ill and until he should get well they had the long days to themselves. When breakfast was over the next morning and the Shepherd had gone with Tam to the hills, Jean decided to wash the clothes. Sandy Crumpet came early, and the two boys went off to play, leaving Jean standing on a stone in the middle of the burn, soaping the clothes and scrubbing them on the flat surface of a rock. The water was so cold it made her arms ache, and she soon decided to let the fast-running stream do the washing for her. She soaped the garments well, weighted them down with stones, and then went to join the boys. She found them flat on their stomachs by the stream, gazing down into a pool of clear water.

"What do you see?" she called out to them.

"Trout," answered Jock, his eyes shining with excitement.

"Let me take a keek," said Jean, flopping down beside them and craning her neck over the edge.

They were all three peering with breathless interest into the water when a strange voice behind them made them jump. For an instant they thought it might be Angus Niel.

"Hello!" said the voice.

The children whirled around, and there before them stood a boy not much older than themselves, but taller and thinner. He had a pale face with large black eyes and dark hair partly covered with a Glengarry bonnet set rakishly over one ear. He wore a suit of gray tweed with plaid-topped stockings, and carried a fishing-rod over his shoulder.

"Hello!" said the stranger again.

"Hello, yourself!" responded Jock.

Jean and Sandy were so relieved to find it wasn't Angus Niel that for an instant they merely gazed at him without speaking.

"What's there?" asked the new boy.

"Fish," said Jock.

"Fish!" cried the new boy, shifting his rod into position. "Where? Let me have a crack at 'em!"

"Na, na, don't be so hasty," cried Jock, heading him off. "You'll get yourself into trouble! Angus Niel would be after you in no time, and if he caught you, he'd cuff your lug for you, and drag you before the bailie for poaching!"

"Who's Angus Niel?" demanded the boy. "I'm not afraid of him."

"Not yet," answered Jock, "but just go on and you will be! He's gamekeeper to the Laird, and he'd rather do for you than not. Aye, he'd just like the feel of you in his fingers, he would." Jock rubbed his ear. "It's but two days gone since he nearly pulled the lug off me because I was running after a rabbit that was eating up our garden. He's terrible suspicious, is Angus, and he's mad at us besides."

"What for?" asked the boy.

"I stepped on him by accident," explained Jock, "and butted him into the burn."

"No wonder he was mad," laughed the boy. "Come on, now. Surely a body can fish. There's no law against that!"

"Well," said Sandy, "law or no law, Angus is against it, and the Auld Laird is terrible particular. He's going to turn out all the farmers in this region and make it into a great game preserve. Nothing else. You're strange hereabouts, I doubt, or you'd ken all this yourself. Where are you from?"

"I'm from London," replied the boy. "I'm staying with Eppie McLean at the castle."

"Are you, now?" gasped Sandy. "Is Eppie your aunt, maybe? She'll be telling you about Angus herself."

"Eppie's not my aunt," said the boy. "She's a friend of my mother, and my mother got her to take me in because I've been sick, and she thought I'd get strong up here, and I'm not going to have my summer spoiled by Angus Niel or any other old bogie man. Stand back now while I cast."

He swung his rod over his head, and the fly fell with a flop in the middle of the pool. He waited a breathless instant while Jock, Sandy, and Jean watched the fly with him, and then, as nothing happened, he cast again. When several such attempts brought no result, he said, "You're sure they 're there?"

"They're lying at the bottom as soft as a baby in a cradle," said Jean. "I could catch them with a skimmer! Gin they don't bite, maybe I'll try it!"

Jock looked at Jean in amazement.

"You're a braw lassie, Jean Campbell," he said severely, "and you just telling about Angus Niel!"

"T'was yourself and Sandy here telling about Angus Niel," Jean answered. "I said nothing at all about him. I'm not afraid of him, either."

"Good for you!" said the new boy with admiration. "You can have a turn with my rod. Try it once before you get the skimmer!"

Jean sprang to her feet and took the rod, though she had never had one like it in her hand before. She made a mighty sweep with it as she had seen the new boy do, but somehow the fly flew off in an unexpected direction and caught in a tree, while the line wound itself in a hopeless snarl around the tip. Jock and Sandy, who had stood by, green with envy, clapped their hands over their mouths and danced with mirth.

"It looks easy," said poor Jean mournfully, "but maybe I'd best stick to the skimmer when I fish."

"Oh, it always does that the first time," said the new boy comfortingly, as he rescued the fly and straightened out the line.

"When a girl tries to do it," added Jock witheringly.

The new boy held out the rod.

"You try it," he said to Jock, and Jock, full of confidence, did not wait for a second invitation.

"Look here, Jean," he said. "This is the way you do it."

He swung the rod with a mighty flourish over his head, bud alas, the fly surprised him too. It caught in Sandy's trousers and surprised Sandy as well. Not only that, it scratched him.

"Ow!" howled Sandy, leaping about like a monkey on the end of the string. "Leave go of me!"

There was a snarl even worse than Jean's, too, and between that and Sandy's jumping about it was some time before the line was disentangled and the hook freed so that Sandy was able to take his turn. Jean, meanwhile, said nothing at all, for Jock looked so crestfallen that she hadn't the heart. When Sandy tried it things were still worse, for the fly flew about so wildly that Jock and Jean fled before it and hid behind some bushes.

"Whoever could catch fish with such gewgaws as them anyway?" said Sandy scornfully, when a second attempt brought no better result. "The fish aren't used to it."

Jock rolled up his sleeves, crept to the side of the burn, and looked over into the pool.

"Hold to me, Sandy," he said, and Sandy immediately sat down on his legs. Then Jock suddenly plunged his arms into the water and before the fish could whisk their tails he had caught one in his hand and thrown it on the grass.

Springing to his feet and upsetting Sandy, he jumped to a rock in the middle of the brook and caught two more. It was now the new boy's turn to be astonished. Apparently Jock had stirred up a whole school of trout, for Sandy, following Jock's lead, also leaped into the stream, and in a few moments six fine trout were flopping about the grass.

"Let's build a fire and cook them," urged the new boy, whose name they soon learned was Alan McRae. "And if old Angus Niel comes nosing around we'll offer him a bite! He can do nothing with four of us, anyway, unless he shoots us, and he'd hang for that. Come on!"

By this time they were all so thrilled with the sport and were having such fun that nobody thought any more about Angus anyway, so Jean ran for a pan, while Jock and Sandy cleaned the fish with Alan's knife, and Alan gathered dry twigs and bracken for the fire. Jean brought down some scones, which she split and spread with butter while the fish were frying. When they were done to a golden brown she put a hot fish on each piece of scone and handed them out to the boys, and when they had eaten every scrap they buried the fish-bones in case Angus should come that way.

After lunch Jean went to wring out the clothes and hang them on the bushes to dry, while Jock and Sandy examined Alan's wonderful book of flies and his reel, and even the creel in which he was to have put the fish, if he had caught any.

"Losh, man!" exclaimed Sandy, swaggering about with his hands in his pockets, "that's all very well. Aye, it's a good game, and you might go dandering along a stream all day playing with it, but if you really want fish, just go after 'em yourself! That's my way. Guddling for trout like you saw me and Jock do, that's the real sport!"

"I believe you," said Alan. "I'm going to try it myself. Come on. Let's go farther up stream and see if we can find another good fishing-hole. I told Eppie I'd bring her a fish to her tea, and I'd hate to go back with nothing at all," and the three boys disappeared in the woods.

Jean finished her work by the brook and went to the house to make more scones, for the picnic had exhausted the supply and they used no other bread. She bustled about the kitchen, mixing, spreading them on the girdle over the fire, keeping the coals bright, and turning them out nicely browned on the mixing-board. She was just finishing the sixth one, when there was a great thumping at the door, and she ran to see what was the matter. There on the doorstep stood the three boys, Alan dripping wet from head to heel, shivering with cold, and with mud and water running from him in streams. Jean threw up her hands.

"It's most michty," she cried, "if I can't ever bake scones in this kitchen without some man body coming in half drowned to mess up my clean floor! However did you go and drop yourself in the burn, Alan McRae? 'Deed and I wonder that your mother lets you go out alone, you're that careless with yourself. And you not long out of a sick bed, too."

"He was guddling for trout," shouted Jock and Sandy in one breath; "and the hole was deep. There was no one sitting on him, and syne over he went!"

Jean seized Alan by the shoulder and drew him into the kitchen, and set him to drip on the hearth while she gave her orders.

"Jock, do you fill the basin with warm water, and you, Sandy, put more peat on the fire. He must have a rinse with hot water and something hot to drink."

"What'll he do for clothes?" cried Jock.

"Dinna fash yourself about clothes," said Jean, rummaging furiously in the "kist." "I'm laying out Father's old kilts he had when he was a boy. He can put them on till his own things are dry. Here's a towel for you," she added, tossing one to Alan. "Rub yourself down well, and when you've dressed, just give a chap at the door, and I'll come in and get you a sup of tea."

Then she disappeared. You can imagine what the kitchen looked like when she came back again. Alan's wet clothes were spread out on her father's chair by the fire, and Alan, gorgeous in his plaid kiltie, was strutting back and forth giving an imitation of the bagpipes on his nose, with Jock and Sandy marching behind him singing "Do ye ken John Peel with his coat so gay" at the top of their lungs.

"Have you gone clean daft?" Jean shouted. "Sit down by the fire and get out of my way while I mop up after you!"

The boys each seized one of the kitchen stools without stopping the song and marched with it to the hearth, and when they came to "Peel's view halloo would awaken the dead," they gave a howl that nearly brought down the ham from the rafters as they banged them down on the hearth-stones. Jean clapped her hands over her ears and ran for the mop, and in no time at all the puddles had disappeared and the boys were drinking tea by the fire.

Of course, Alan had no shoes to put on because his were soaking wet, and as it was now late in the afternoon it began to be a question how he should get back to the castle. It was still cold for going barefoot, and he was not used to it besides, and his clothes certainly would not be fit to put on for a long time. They held a consultation. Alan thought he could go without shoes.

"You'll do nothing of the kind," said Jean firmly. "What sickness was it you had, anyway?"

"Measles," said Alan, looking ashamed of it.

"Measles!" shouted Sandy. "That's naught but a baby disease. My little sister had that. Sal, but I've had worse things the matter with me! I've had the fever, and once I cut my toe with the axe!"

"Hold your tongue, Sandy," said Jean, "and dinna boast! If Alan's had measles he can't go back to the castle barefoot; so you must just be stepping yourself, and stop by at the castle to tell Eppie McLean that Alan will bide here till his things are dry."

Sandy rose reluctantly and set down his empty mug.

"Well, then, if I must, I must," he said, and started off down the hill whistling.

V. EVENING IN THE WEE BIT HOOSIE

When he was out of sight, Jean brought in the washing and then it was time to get supper. Alan helped set the table and kept the fire bright under the pot, while Jock fed the hens and brought in the eggs; and when the Shepherd and Tam returned from the hills, you can imagine how surprised they were to find three children waiting for them instead of two. At supper the Shepherd had to be told all the adventures of the day and how it happened that Alan was wearing the kilts, and by the time it was over you would have thought they had known each other all their lives. While Jean cleared away the dishes, the Shepherd drew his chair to the fire and beckoned Alan to him.

"Come here, laddie," he said, "and give us a look at your plaidie. It's been lying there in the kist, and I've not seen a sight of it since I was a lad. It's the Campbell plaid, ye ken, and I mind once when I was a lad I was on my way home from the kirk and a hare crossed my path. It's ill luck for a hare to cross your path, and fine I proved it. I clean forgot it was the Sabbath and louped the dyke after him. My kiltie caught on a stone, and there I was hanging upside down. My father loosed me, but my kiltie was torn and I had to go to bed without my supper for breaking the Sabbath."

"Is the hole there yet?" asked Jean.

"Na, na;" said the Shepherd. "You didn't think your grandmother was such a thriftless wifie as that! She mended the hole so that you could never find where it had been."

He examined fold after fold carefully.

"There, now," he exclaimed at last, "if you want to see mending that would make you proud to wear it, look at that."

Jean and Jock stuck their heads over his shoulder, and Alan twisted himself nearly in two trying to see his own back.

"We have a plaid a good deal like this," said Alan, looking closely at the pattern. "My mother's name was McGregor, but she has relations named Campbell."

"Are you really a Scotch body, then?" cried Robin with new interest in Alan. "I thought you were an English boy."

"I live in London," Alan answered, "but my mother's people are all Scotch, and she loves Scotland. That's one reason why she sent me up here to be with Eppie McLean."

"Losh, mannie," cried the Shepherd, "if you have Campbell relatives and your mother's name was McGregor, it's likely you are a descendant from old Rob Roy himself, and if so, we're all kinsmen. Inversnaid, where Rob Roy's cave is, is but a few miles from here, and it was in this very country that he hid himself among rocks and caves, giving to the poor with his left hand what he took from the rich with his right. Well, well, laddie, the old clans are scattered now, but blood is thicker than water still, and you're welcome to the fireside of your kinsman!"

"Is he really a relation?" cried Jean and Jock eagerly.

"Well," said the Scotchman cautiously, "I'm not saying he is precisely, but I'm not saying he is not, either. The Campbells and the McGregors have lived in these parts for better than two hundred years, and it's not likely that Alan could lay claim to both names and be no relation at all. If there were still clans, as there used to be in the old days, we'd all belong to the same one, and that I do not doubt."

"I'm sure I'd like that," said Alan, and Jock was so delighted with his new relative that he stood on his head in the middle of the floor to express his feelings. When the excitement had died down a bit, Alan drew his stool up beside the Shepherd's knee and said: "Won't you please tell us about Rob Roy, Cousin Campbell? If he's an ancestor of mine, I ought to know more about him."

"Oh, do, Father," echoed the Twins, planting their stools beside the other knee. Even Tam was interested. He sat on the hearth in front of the Shepherd, looking up into his face as if he understood every word.

The Shepherd gazed thoughtfully into the fire for a moment; then he said: "I can tell you what my grandsire told me, and he got it from his grandsire, so it must be true. In the beginning Rob Roy was as staunch a man as any, and held his own property like other gentlemen. Craig Royston was the name of his place, and fine and proud he was of it, too. He was a gey shrewd man in the cattle-dealing, and his neighbor, the Duke of Montrose, thinking to benefit his own estate, lent Rob money to set him up in the trade. There was a pawky rascal named McDonald who was partner to Rob, and didn't he run away with the money, leaving Rob in debt to the Duke and nothing to pay him with? The Duke foreclosed on Rob at once, and took away Craig Royston and added it to his own estate. You can well believe that Rob was not the man to take such dealings with patience. If the Duke had not been so hasty, Rob would more than likely have got hold of McDonald and made him pay either out of his purse or out of his skin, but he did neither the one nor the other. Instead he left his home and took his clan with him into the mountains and became the terror of the whole country-side."

"Wasn't he a good man?" asked Jean, gazing at her father with round eyes.

"Well," said the Shepherd, "not just what you'd call pious, maybe, and it cannot be said that he was aye regular at the kirk. It's true he never forgot an enemy, but he never forgot a kindness either and was loyal and true to them that were true to him."

"What did he do when they weren't true to him?" asked Jock.

"He made them wish they had been," replied the Shepherd mildly.

"But what made the Duke of Montrose take away Craig Royston?" asked Jock. "Didn't he have a great big place of his own?"

"Aye," answered Robin, "but what difference does that make? The more land he had, the more land he wanted, the same as other lairds. Be that as it may, Craig Royston was certainly taken away from Rob, and a bitter man it made of him."

"Why, it's just like ourselves and the Auld Laird," cried Jean. "He's going to take away our home from us!"

"It's not just the same, little woman," said the Shepherd, laying his big brown hand on Jean's small one on his knee. "But the loss of it hurts just the same. Rob Roy loved Craig Royston no better than we love this wee bit hoosie."

"But why must you go, then?" asked Alan, his eyes shining with interest and sympathy.

"You see; lad," answered the Shepherd, "it's like the tale of the dog in the manger. The Auld Laird will neither use the land nor let us." He explained about the lease, and when he had finished, Alan said, "But what will you do when you leave this place?"

"I'm spiering the same question myself," answered the Shepherd. "As yet I dinna ken."

"I tell you what," shouted Jock, springing to his feet and knocking over his stool. "Why don't we live in the caves the way Rob Roy did? If the Crumpets and all the people who have to give up their homes should band together in a clan and hide themselves in the glen, the Auld Laird could send all the Mr. Craigies and Angus Niels in the world after us and they'd never get us!"

The Shepherd smiled and shook his head. "The time for that has gone by," he said sadly. "Na, na, we must just submit. But one thing I do know, and that is, we'll not seek a place with the Laird of Kinross. They say he will let his land to none but members of the Established Church, and I'll not give up my religion for any man not if I'm forever walking the world!"

"But come, now," he went on, seeing them downcast, "you all have faces on you as long as a summer Sabbath. Cheer up, and I'll tell you a tale my grandfather told me of the water cow of Loch Leven. You mind the song says, 'The Campbells are coming from bonnie Loch Leven.' Well, it was around that loch that the Campbells pastured their cattle. One day when my grandsire was a young lad he was playing with some other children on the pastures near the shore, when all of a sudden what should they see among their own cows but a fine young dun-colored heifer without any horns. She was lying by herself on the green grass, chewing her cud and looking so gentle and pretty that the children played around her without fear. They wound a wreath of daisies and put it on her neck, and then they got on her back. The cow stretched out longer and longer to make room for them until they were all on her back except my grandsire. Then all of a sudden the dun cow rose up, first on her hind legs, tipping the children all forward, and then on her forelegs tipping them all back ward, yet no one fell off at all, and when she was up on her feet, didn't she start straight away for the deep waters of the loch? The children screamed and tried to get off her back, but no matter how hard they tried, there they stuck. My grandsire ran screaming toward them, and put up his hand to pull them down, and his finger touched the dun cow's back! Now never believe me, if his finger didn't stick so he could not pull it away, and by that he knew the dun heifer for a water cow and that she had bewitched the children. He was being dragged along with them toward the water, when all of a sudden he slipped out his knife and with one blow chopped off his own finger and he was wanting that finger till the day of his death."

"What became of the others?" gasped Alan, his black eyes glowing like coals.

"They went on the dun cow's back into the lake, and the water closed over them and they were never seen again," said the Shepherd, "and that's the end of the tale."

While the Shepherd talked, the twilight had deepened into darkness, the fire had died down, and the corners of the room were filled with mysterious tricky shadows that danced with the flickering flames on the hearth. Jean looked fearfully over her shoulder. There was a creepy feeling in the back of her neck, and Jock's eyes were as round as door-knobs. The Shepherd laughed at them.

"Good children have little to fear from the fairy folk," he said. "Come, now, your eyes are fair sticking out of your heads. I'll give you a skirl on the bagpipes if Jeanie'll bring them from the closet. Jock, stir up the fire, and Alan, give your clothes a turn and see if they are drying."

The children ran to do these errands, and in a moment the fire was flaming gayly up the chimney, chasing the murky shadows out of the corners and making the room bright and cheerful again, while the Shepherd, tucking the bag under his arm, stirred the echoes on old Ben Vane with the wild strains of "Bonnie Doon" and "Over the Water to Charlie." At last he struck up the music of the Highland Fling, and the three children sprang to the middle of the floor and danced the wild Scotch dance together.

Just as the fun was at its height, and Alan, looking very handsome in his kilts, was doing the heel and toe with great energy, there came a loud rap at the door. Instantly everything stopped, just as short as Cinderella's ball did when the clock struck twelve, and the Shepherd, laying aside his bagpipes, opened the door. There stood a man with a bundle on his arm. "Eppie McLean sent these clothes to the lad," he said, handing the bundle to the Shepherd, "and he's to come back along with me." Alan took the bundle, thanked the man, and disappeared with Jock into "the room," where he changed his clothes, returning the kilts, with regret, to Jock. "I've had just a grand day," he said to Jean and the Shepherd as he shook hands and took leave of them in the kitchen afterward. "I'll be back to-morrow for my clothes."

"Come back and play then," said Jock.

When he was gone, Jean folded the kilts away in the closet again. "He's a fine braw laddie," said the Shepherd.

"Aye," said Jock. "He had two suits of clothes, one as good as the other, but he was not proud."

"I wonder what his father's work is," said Jean.

"He never spoke of his father at all, just his mother," said Jock, and at that moment the wag-at-the-wall clock struck nine.

"Havers!" said Jean. "Look at the hour, Jock Campbell! Get you to your bed."

VI. TWO DISCOVERIES

That night Jock dreamed of water cows, and clans dressed in kilts, and when Sandy appeared the next morning, his head was still buzzing with wild schemes of adventure.

"Come awa', Sandy," he said, "let's explore. We'll go up the burn and see if we can't find out where it begins."

"What'll we do for lunch?" asked Sandy, who was practical. "I brought a scone with me—but it'll never be enough for two."

"Ho!" said Jock. "If Rob Roy and all his men could live in caves all the time and take care of themselves, I guess we can do it for one day. We can fish, and maybe we might find some birds' eggs. I'm not afraid."

"What about Alan?" asked Jean.

"If he comes to play, tell him to follow us right up the burn and keep whistling the pewit's call three times over, and if we don't see him, we'll hear him," said Jock. "There's no danger of not finding us if he follows the water," and he and Sandy set forth at once.

Jean had finished her work and was wondering what to do with the long day which stretched before her, when Alan came running up the hill and burst into the kitchen.

"Look here what I've got, Jean," he said, thumping a parcel down on the kitchen table and tearing it open. "Eppie put this up for me."

Jean looked and there was a whole pound of bacon, three big scones, and a dozen eggs. "Save us!" cried Jean, clasping her hands in admiration. "What will you do with it all?"

"I'll show you!" said Alan. "Where's Jock?"

"He and Sandy have gone up the burn, exploring," said Jean. "They said you were to follow, and if you didn't find them, keep whistling the pewit's call three times till they answered you."

"What is the pewit's call?" asked Alan.

"Michty me!" said Jean. "Think of not knowing that!" She pursed up her lips and whistled "Pee-wit, pee-wit, pee-wit."

"You see, we don't have them in London;" Alan apologetically explained, "unless it's in the Zoo; but I say, Jean, aren't you coming, too? You're as good as a boy any day. Come along!"

"All right," said Jean. "I wanted to dreadfully. I'll get a basket for the lunch." She went to the closet and brought out a basket which her father had made out of split willow twigs, packed the lunch in it, and off they started.

They passed the place where the fish-bones were buried, and the spot where Alan had fallen into the water the day before, and then plunged into the deep pine forest which filled the glen and covered the mountain-sides. The pine-needles lay thick on the ground, and above them the pine boughs waved in the breeze, making a soft sighing sound, "like a giant breathing," Jean said. The silence deepened as they went farther and farther into the woods. There was only the purring of the water, the occasional snapping of a twig, or the lonely cry of a bird to break the stillness. It was dark, too, except where the sunshine, breaking through the thick branches overhead, made spots of golden light upon the pine-needles.

"It's almost solemn; isn't it?" said Jean to Alan in a hushed voice. "I was never so far in the woods before."

"I wonder which side of the burn the boys went. If we should take the wrong side, we might not find them," said Alan.

"Let's whistle," said Jean. She puckered her lips and gave the pewit call, but there was no answer.

"Perhaps they didn't hear it because the burn makes such a noise. It keeps growing louder and louder," said Alan.

Whistling and listening for an answer at every few steps, they climbed over rocks and fallen trees, keeping as close as possible to the stream, until suddenly they found themselves gazing up at a beautiful waterfall which came gushing from a pile of giant rocks reaching up among the topmost boughs of the pines.

"Oh, it's bonny! but how shall we get up?" cried Jean.

"We must just find a way," said Alan.

"It's a grand place for robbers and poachers," said Jean, looking fearsomely at the cliffs stretching far above them. "Angus Niel says the forests are full of them."

"I'd as soon meet a poacher as Angus Niel himself," said Alan, laughing, "but I'm not afraid as long as you're with me. It's Angus that's afraid of you, Jock says."

Jean laughed too. "I'm not afraid when I'm in my own kitchen, but it's different in the woods," she said.

Alan had been nosing around among the rocks as they talked, getting nearer and nearer to the fall, and now he suddenly disappeared, and for a few moments Jean was quite alone in the woods. Soon Alan reappeared from behind the fall itself and beckoned her to follow him.

Jean was looking at the wall of rock which loomed above them. "Sal!" she remarked, "we'll be needing wings to get up there, or we'll smash all the eggs for sure."

For answer Alan popped out of sight again behind the fall, and Jean, following closely in his wake, was just in time to catch sight of his legs as he dived into a hole opening into the rocky wall. The cliff from which the water plunged overhung the rocks below in such a way that she could pass behind the veil of water without getting wet at all.

Into this mysterious opening behind the fall Jean followed her leader, and found herself climbing a narrow dry channel through which the stream had once forced its way. It was a hard, rough scramble up a narrow passage worn by the water and through holes almost too small to squeeze through, but at last she saw Alan's heels just disappearing over the edge of a jutting rock and knew they were coming out into daylight again. An instant later Alan's head appeared in the opening, his hand reached down to help her up, and with one last effort she came out upon an open ledge and looked about her.

She could not help an exclamation of delight at what she saw. The rock was so high that they could look out over the treetops clear to the slope where the little gray house stood. The waterfall, plunging from a still higher level, made a barrier on one side of them, and on the other side the cliff rose, a sheer wall of rock. Between the wall of water and the wall of rock there was a cave extending into the solid rock for a distance of about twenty feet. There was absolutely no way of reaching this fastness except through the hidden stair, and one might wander for years through the forest and never see it at all.

"Oh," exclaimed Jean, "it's wonderful! How Jock will love this place! Don't you believe this very cave was used by Rob Roy and his men?" and Alan, swelling with pride to think he had found it all himself, said yes, he was sure of it.

"I tell you what we'll do," cried Alan, a minute later. "We'll just leave the basket here in the cave, and when we've found the boys we'll come back and have our lunch here."

They tucked the basket away out of sight on a rocky shelf in the cave, and found their way down the steep rough stairway to the bed of the stream again and, making a wide detour, came out above the fall. They struggled on for nearly a mile farther still without finding any trace of the boys, and were beginning to be discouraged, when they saw a break in the trees with glimpses of blue sky beyond, and a few moments later came out upon the shores of a tiny mountain lake, shining like a beautiful blue jewel in the dark setting of the pine trees on its banks.

Beyond the lake the purple peaks of higher mountains made a ragged outline against the sky. The sun was now almost directly overhead; the waters of the lake were still, and its lovely shores were mirrored on the placid surface. A great eagle soared in stately circles in the deep blue sky. It was so beautiful and so still that the children stood a moment among the rocks where the tarn emptied itself into the mountain stream to look at it.

"It's just the place for a water cow, or a horse maybe," Jean whispered to Alan.

"Sh!" was Alan's only reply. He seized Jean's hand and dragged hear down behind a rock and pointed toward the south. There, coming out of the woods, was a beautiful stag. It poised its noble head, and sniffed the air, as if it suspected there might be human beings about, and then stepped daintily to the lake-shore and bent to drink. Its lips had scarcely touched the water when the children were startled by the loud report of a gun.

"Poachers," gasped Jean, hiding her face and wishing they had never come. "Oh, where are Jock and Sandy?" Her only thought was to make herself as small as possible and keep out of sight behind the rocks, but Alan peered through the screen of bushes which hid the rock and made violent gestures to Jean to make her look, too. Jean crawled on her hands and knees to Alan's side, and when she looked, what she saw made her so angry that she would have sprung to her feet if Alan had not held her down with a fierce grip. The stag was lying by the lake-shore, and a man with the muzzle of his gun still smoking was running toward it from the woods. The man was Angus Niel!

Jean was so astonished that for an instant she could not believe her own eyes. The two children flattened themselves out on their stomachs and watched him pull a boat from its hiding-place among some bushes on the shore, paddle quietly to the spot where the dead stag lay, and load it swiftly into the boat. Then he raced back to the woods again and reappeared, carrying a string of dead rabbits. These also he crowded into the boat, and then, taking up the oars, rowed across the lake to a landing-place on the other side. The children watched him, scarcely breathing in their excitement, until he had unloaded his game from the boat and disappeared into the woods, dragging the body of the stag after him. In a few moments he came back for the rabbits and, having disposed of them in the same mysterious way, returned to the boat.

Then Jean exploded in a fierce whisper. "The old thief!" she said, shaking her fist after him. "He's the poacher himself! That's why he never brings any one before the bailie, though he's always telling about catching them at it! And he making such a fuss because Jock chased the rabbit that was eating up our garden! Oh, oh, oh!"

She clutched Alan and shook him in her boiling indignation. Alan laughed and shook her back. "I didn't do it, you little spitfire!" he whispered, and Jean moaned, "Oh, I know it, Alan, but I can't catch him and I'm so angry I've just got to do something to somebody."

"Do you know what that old thief does?" said Alan. "He sends that game down to the city—to Glasgow, or Edinburgh, or even London, maybe—and gets a lot of money for it! No wonder he tells big stories to make people afraid to go into the woods."

"I hope he won't meet the boys," moaned Jean. "Jock would be sure to let his tongue loose, and then maybe he'd shoot him too!"

"Listen," said Alan. He gave the pewit's call and waited. It was answered from a point so near that they were startled. They looked in every direction but saw nothing of the boys.

"Maybe it was a real pewit after all," whispered Jean, but just then a tiny pebble struck Alan's cap, and, looking around in the direction from which it came, he saw two freckled faces rise up from behind the rock on the opposite side of the spring.

"There they are," he said, punching Jean and pointing; "they came up the other side of the burn." Then, making a cup of his hands, he called across the stream, "Did you see him?" The boys nodded. "Slip back as fast as you can down that side of the burn," Alan said, "and we'll meet at the fall. Wait at the foot if you get there first. We've got something to show you. Whist, and be quick, for he'll be coming back before long, and this way like as not."

Jock and Sandy nodded and disappeared, and Alan and Jean, springing from their hiding-place, hurried as fast as they could down their side of the stream to the trysting-place.

VII. THE CLAN

When Jean and Alan reached the waterfall, they found Jock and Sandy there before them. "Come over to our side," Alan called. The two boys ran further down stream and crossed the brook on stones which stood out of the water, and in a moment more were back again at the foot of the fall.

"What have you got to show us?" demanded Jock. "I hope it's something to eat." Jock had bitterly regretted his morning decision to find his food in the forest. The scone which Sandy had brought from home had been divided and eaten long ago; and all four of the children were now so hungry that they could think of nothing else, not even of Angus Niel and their adventures by the lake.

Alan looked cautiously around in every direction. "Follow me, and keep quiet tongues in your heads," he said. Then he disappeared under the fall, and Jean instantly followed him. For a moment Jock and Sandy were as mystified as Jean had been when Alan first found the secret stairway, but it was not long before they, too, saw the hole in the rock, plunged in and, following the winding passage-way, came out upon the top of the rock.

"There," said Alan, beaming with pride, as he displayed his wonderful lair, "doesn't this beat Robinson Crusoe all to pieces? If he had found a place like this on his desert island, he wouldn't have had to build a stockade or anything."

"It's one of the very caves where Rob Roy hid! I'm sure of it," Jock declared with conviction, and Sandy was so overcome with admiration that he turned a back somersault and almost upset Jean, who was coming out of the cave with the basket on her arm.

"You see," said Alan, "we could stay here a week if we had food enough, and never come down at all. All we'd have to do for water would be to hold a pan under the edge of the fall. There's no way of getting up here except by the secret stair, and that's not easy to find. There never was such a place for fun."

Sandy had righted himself by this time and was gazing ecstatically at the basket, which Jean had begun to unpack. "Losh!" he cried. "Look, Jock!

Bacon and eggs and scones! Oh, my word!" Jock gave one look and whooped for joy.

"Keep still," said Alan. "Angus may be coming back this way, and he has a gun with him. We're safe enough up here, if we keep quiet, but if you go howling around like that, he'll surely hunt for the noise."

For a moment they kept quiet and listened, but there was no sound except the noise of the falling waters. "Huh!" Sandy snorted, "he couldn't hear anything, anyway. The roar of the fall hides all the other noises."

"Oh, let's eat!" begged Jock, caressing his empty stomach and gazing longingly at the food.

"You can't eat now," said Jean; "the food must be cooked first, and what shall we do for a fire?"

"We could make one right here on the rock," said Alan, "if we had something to burn. I've got matches."

"We'll have to get twigs and dry pine-needles and broken branches," said Jock, "and bring them up the secret stair, though it'll be hard work getting them through the narrow places. We ought to have a rope. We could pull a basketful up over the edge of the rock as easy as nothing."

"We'll bring a rope next time," said Alan. "Hurry! I'm starving!"

The three boys disappeared down the secret stair, and while they were gone, Jean found loose stones, with which she made a support for the frying-pan around a space for the fire. The boys were soon back with plenty of small fuel, and in a short time a bright fire was blazing on the rock and there was a wonderful smell of frying bacon in the air. The boys sat cross-legged around the fire, while Jean turned the bacon and broke the eggs into the sputtering fat.

"You look just exactly like Tam watching the rabbit-hole," laughed Jean. "I wonder you don't paw the ground and bark!"

At last the scones were handed out, each one laden with a slice of bacon and a fried egg, and there was blissful silence for some moments.

"Oh, aren't you glad you didn't die of the measles and miss this?" Sandy said to Alan, rolling over on his back and waving his legs in the air as he finished his third egg. Alan's mouth was too full for a reply other than a cordial grunt.

"Why, Sandy Crumpet!" exclaimed Jean, reprovingly, "don't you believe heaven is nicer than Scotland?"

"Maybe it is," Sandy admitted, doubtfully, "but I like this better than sitting around playing on harps and trumpets the way the angels do."

"Sandy Crumpet played the trumpet," howled Jock in derision. "Indeed and indeed, Sandy, I like this better than having to hear you." Then, before Sandy could think of an answer a memory of the catechism crossed his mind, and he added as afterthought, "How do you ken you're one of the elect, anyway, Sandy Crumpet? If you're not, you'd not be playing on any trumpets, or harps either, but like as not frying in the hot place like that bacon there."

Sandy rushed to the defense of his character. "I'm just as elect as you are, Jock Campbell," he said.

This time Jock had no answer ready, and Jean reproved them both. "Shame on you!" she said. "You'll neither one of you get so much as a taste of heaven, I doubt, and you talking like that."

"Where will Angus Niel be going, then, when he dies?" asked Jock. "I don't just mind whether there's a chance for thieves, but the Bible says drunkards and such-like stand no chance at all."

"It's not for us to judge," said Jean primly, "but I have my opinion."

Alan had been busily eating during this conversation, and now he joined in. "I say," he began, "I'm not worrying about what will become of Angus Niel after he's dead. I want to know what's going to be done with him right now. We're the only ones that know about this. Are we just going to keep whist, or shall we tell on him?"

"Let's tell on him!" shouted Sandy.

"Who'll you be telling?" said Jean with some scorn.

"Why, the bailie, maybe, or the Auld Laird himself," said Sandy.

"Havers!" said Jean. "You're a braw lad to go hobnobbing with the bailie. He'll not believe you, anyway; he's a friend of Angus himself, and, as for the Auld Laird, how would you get hold of him at all, and he far away in London?"

Sandy subsided, crushed, and then Jock had a bright idea. "I tell you what we'll do," he cried, springing to his feet. "Let's have a clan, like Rob Roy, and we'll just badger the life out of Angus Niel. We'll never let him know who we are, but keep kim forever stepping and give him no rest. If he thinks somebody's following him up all the time, he'll not sleep easy o' nights!"

This suggestion was greeted with riotous applause. "He'd not sleep easy if he knew Jean was after him, I'll go bail," laughed Alan.

"Hooray!" shouted Sandy, waving his legs frantically. "What shall we call it?"

"Let's call it the Rob Roy Clan," said Alan.

"Hooray!" roared Sandy again.

"If we're a Clan, we'll have to have a chief," said Jean, "and if the Chief bids us do anything, we'll just have to do it. That's the way it was in the real Rob Roy Clan. Father said so."

"Jock thought of it first. Let him be Chief," said Alan.

"No!" cried Jean promptly. "Are you thinking I'll put my head in a bag like that, and he my own brother? 'Deed, I'd never get a lick of work out of him on Saturday if I did! Na, na, lads! Whoever's Chief, it won't be Jock."

"Maybe you'd like to be the Chief yourself," retorted Jock, "but it's enough to be bossed by you at home! Besides, whoever heard of a girl being Chief, anyway?"

"Alan can be Chief," said Jean, and so the matter was settled.

"If I'm Chief," said Alan, "you'll all have to swear an oath of fealty to me."

"What's an oath of fealty?" Jock demanded suspiciously, and Jean added in a shocked voice, "Alan, you'd never be asking us to take the name of the Lord in vain!"

"It's not that kind of an oath," laughed Alan. "You just have to vow to obey the Chief in everything." Then an idea popped into his head. "In a real Clan they are all kinsmen, but here's Sandy, and he's neither Campbell nor McGregor. We'll have to make a blood brother of him before he can join."

"What's a blood brother? How do you make 'em?" asked Sandy.

"I'll show you," said Alan. He drew his knife from his pocket and while the other three watched him in breathless admiration, he made a little cut in his wrist and immediately passed the knife to Jock. "You do the same," he commanded.

Jock obeyed his Chief and passed the knife to Jean, who promptly followed his example.

"Now, Sandy," said Alan.

Sandy hated the sight of blood, and he was a little pale under his freckles as he shut his eyes and jabbed himself gingerly with the point. Then Alan took a drop of blood from each wrist and mingled them with a drop from Sandy's.

"Now, Sandy," he said, as he stirred the compound into a gory paste, "you repeat after me, 'My foot is on my native heath, my name it is McGregor.'" Sandy obeyed with solemnity, and, this important ceremony over, Alan pronounced him a member of the Clan in good and regular standing.

Then, by the Chief's orders, Jean, Jock, and Sandy, each in turn placed their hands under Alan's hand, while they promised to obey him without question in all matters pertaining to the Clan.

"Only," said Jean, "you mustn't tell us to do anything wrong."

"I won't," promised Alan. And so the Rob Roy Clan came into being.

Alan took command at once. "We must have a sign," he said. "Just like Clan Alpine in 'The Lady of the Lake.' Go, my henchmen," he cried, striking a noble attitude, and waving his hand toward the forest, "bring hither sprays of the Evergreen Pine, and we'll stick 'em in our bonnets just like Roderick Dhu and his men. Roderick Vich Alpine Dhu, ho! iero!"

The two boys instantly disappeared down the hole in the rock on this errand, leaving Jean and Alan to guard the cave.

VIII. THE POACHERS

While all these things were happening, Angus Niel had returned from his errand across the little lake, and was making his way slowly toward home, following the course of the stream. As he came near the fall he stopped and sniffed. There was certainly a most appetizing smell of bacon in the air!

"It can't be!" he said aloud to himself. He sniffed again, and his face turned purple with rage. "Meat," he snorted, "as I live! The bold rascals! Poaching in broad daylight and cooking their game right under my nose!" It wasn't under his nose at all, of course, for the rock was far above him, and it wasn't game either.

"I'll soon cure them of that trick," he muttered, as he climbed silently over the rocks and gazed searchingly about. It was not long before he caught sight of a thin curl of blue smoke rising from the top of the rock.

"Aha!" he growled under his breath, "I've got you now, my bold gentlemen! I'll teach you to flaunt your thefts in the face of the Laird's own gamekeeper, once I get my hands on you!" At once he began nosing about the rocks in search of the path by which the poachers had climbed the cliff.

Meanwhile Sandy and Jock had found the sprays of the Evergreen Pine and were on their way back to the cave with them, when Jock suddenly seized Sandy by the arm and ducked down behind a boulder. There, not a hundred feet away, stood Angus Niel gazing up at the top of the rock! His back was toward them, and the noise of the waterfall had drowned out the sound of voices, or they surely would not have escaped his notice. As it was, they slipped behind the fall, whisked into the hole, and began climbing the secret stair like two frightened squirrels. An instant later they startled Alan and Jean, who were in the cave, by dashing in after them on all fours.

"What on earth is the matter?" cried Jean.

"Matter, indeed!" gasped Jock, out of breath. "Angus Niel is down there, and he's seen the smoke! He almost saw us, but we just gave him the slip and got by."

"Keep out of sight, all of you," commanded the Chief, "and leave him to me."

The obedient Clan flattened themselves against the back of the cave, while Alan crept to the edge of the rock on his stomach like a lizard, and, lying there, was able to peep through the thick screen of leaves and see what was going on below. The gamekeeper was still scrambling over the rocks and looking, as Alan said afterward, "for all the world like a dog who had lost the trail and was trying to find it again."

As the lookout was well screened, Alan soon allowed the rest of the Clan to join him, and Angus Niel little guessed, as he prowled about over the rocks, that every move was watched from above. Despairing of finding the path, he decided at last to get up a tree and make an observation. He selected a large pine which grew near the cave and began to climb.

So long as he stood on the ground, the children knew it was impossible for Angus to see them, but when he began to climb, they scuttled back into the cave as fast as they could go.

Climbing is hard work for a fat man, and the gamekeeper found himself covered with pitch before he had gone more than halfway up, but he puffed on in spite of difficulties and at last reached a point from which he could look directly across the surface of the rock, but from which the cave was entirely hidden behind a projection in the wall of the cliff.

Angus saw what he supposed to be the whole shelf of the rock, and he saw that there was no one there. He could see the fire and the frying-pan, the egg shells lying about, and even the portion of bacon that Jean had not cooked. They were all in full view, but apparently the poachers had gone away into the woods, leaving their airy camp deserted. There was no one there; of that he felt, certain.

"I'll just give 'em a surprise," thought the gamekeeper to himself. "If they found a way up, I can, too. I'll help myself to a snack of that bacon, and if they come back and find me—well, I have my gun with me and I don't like being interrupted at my meals."

He backed down the tree like a fat cat, and made a desperate search for the path, and this time he actually succeeded in finding it. He chuckled to himself as he plunged into the passage and began to climb. He had gone about a third of the way up, when he reached the narrowest point of the channel and tried to force himself through, but the space was so small that no matter how much he tried, he could not get by. His gun was in his way too, but he could not leave it below, as that would be putting it into the hands of the poachers if they should return too soon.

In vain he twisted and squirmed, he could get no farther, and moreover he was afraid the gun might go off by accident in his struggles. When he found that he could not possibly go up, he decided to go down; but he found, to his horror, that he couldn't do that either. There he stuck, and an angrier man than Angus Niel it would have been hard to find. A projecting rock punched him in the stomach, and when he pressed back against the rock behind him, to free himself, he scraped the skin off his back. Casting prudence to the winds, he howled with pain and rage, and the sound, carried up through the narrow passage, echoed in the cave like the roar of a lion.

The children, meanwhile, had kept in hiding, and when they heard these blood-curdling sounds, they at first did not know what caused them, because, of course, they could not see what was happening below, but they knew very soon that they were not made by a wild animal because wild animals do not swear.

"It's Angus, stuck in the secret stairway," Alan said, smothering his laughter. "He's too fat to get through!" He crept to the edge and peeped down the hole. There, far below, he could see the top of Angus's head and the muzzle of his gun.

The Chief was a boy of great presence of mind. He backed hastily away from the hole and ran to the fall, snatching up the pan as he passed. This he filled with water and, rushing back, he instantly sent a small deluge down upon the head of the hapless Angus.

The gamekeeper was dumbfounded by this new attack. Had he not with his own eyes seen that the rocky shelf was empty? How, then, could this thing be? He rolled his eyes upward, but there was no one in sight. He had heard all his life tales of witches and water cows, of spells cast upon people by fairies, of their being borne away by them into mountain caverns and held as prisoners for years and years; and he made up his mind that such a fate had now befallen him.

Firmly convinced that he was the victim of enchantment, he became palsied with terror, arid began to plead with the unseen tormentors who he believed held him in thrall. "Only leave me loose, dear good little people," he howled, "and I'll never, never trouble you more!"

At this point Alan, shaking with mirth, sent down another panful of water, and Angus, redoubling his efforts, wrenched himself free, scraping off quantities of skin as he did so. They could hear him scuttling down the secret stair as fast as his legs would carry him, and when he emerged below, they watched him hurry away through the forest, casting fearful glances over his shoulder as he ran. Alan made a hollow of his two hands and sent after him a wild note, like the wailing of a banshee.

"Angus Niel, Angus Niel," rose the piercing note, "bring back my beautiful stag, my stag that lived by the tarn!"

As the sound reached his ears, Angus redoubled his speed, and they could hear him crashing through the underbrush as if the devil himself were really at his heels.

When the sounds died away in the distance, the Rob Roy Clan rolled on the floor of the cave with laughter.

"There!" said Alan, as he sat up and wiped his eyes. "That'll fix Angus Niel! We've scared him out of a year's growth, and he'll never dare meddle with this place again. Come on, now. It's time to go home, but to-morrow we'll come back and fix this place up in a way that would make Robinson Crusoe green with envy."

They carefully put water on the ashes of their fire, stuck the sprigs of Evergreen Pine in their bonnets, and sped down the secret stairway and home.

IX. A RAINY DAY

The next morning, as she was finishing the beds, Jean heard the pewit call and at once knew that the Clan was abroad. She ran to the door, and the three boys came in together,—Jock from the garden, where he had been pulling weeds in the potato-patch, and Sandy and Alan from the road. They were carrying a large basket, and Sandy was laden down with a coil of rope in addition.

"What have you got there?" demanded Jean.

"Stores for the Cave," said Alan, "and a rope to let down from the rock. Come on; let's go as soon as we can, for it looks like rain and we've got a lot to do to get the cave ready for wet weather."

"Where did you get 'em?" asked Jock, eyeing the basket with interest and wondering what was inside.

"Oh," said Alan, "I just asked Eppie. She lets me have anything I want. My mother told her to stuff me while I'm here, and if I take the food off to the woods with me she doesn't have to cook it at home, so she's suited, and I am, too."

Jean hastily gathered together a few cooking utensils, and a few minutes later the four set forth, carrying the provisions and wearing proudly in their bonnets the sprig of pine, the insignia of the Clan. The sky was downcast and the woods seemed dark and gloomy as they made their way toward the waterfall.

"What'll we do if it rains?" cried Sandy. "It's no such fine thing just sitting still in a cave."

"I've a plan in my head," said the Chief. "Wait and see."

As they reached the fall, Alan sent Sandy and Jock to gather wood, while Jean guarded the basket at the foot of the rock and he himself darted up the secret stairway with the rope. From the top he let down the rope and Jean fastened it through the handles of the basket. Alan then drew it up, emptied the contents, and sent back the basket for the wood which Sandy and Jock had by that time collected.

They all worked as swiftly as possible, for the woods were growing darker and darker every minute and they could now hear the roll of thunder above the noise of the waterfall. They had gathered and sent up six basketfuls, when the rain came splashing down in earnest, and the Clan scrambled up the secret stair and into the cave for shelter. Alan had piled the wood in the cave as fast as he had pulled it up, and there was now a fine pile of dry fuel.

"Sandy, you build the fire," commanded the Chief, seating himself on the wood-pile.

"The rain will put it out," said Sandy.

"Make it in the cave," said Alan.

"Then the smoke will put us out," cried Jean.

"Try it and see," said Alan. "We can't have lunch without a fire, for I've brought mealy puddings."

"Mealy puddings!" cried Sandy, licking his lips, and he went to work with a will. Fortunately the wind blew from the east, so they were not absolutely choked by the smoke, and soon the fire was burning briskly; making a spot of flaming color against the dark background of the cave. Jock ran to the fall and filled the pan with water, and soon the mealy puddings were bobbing merrily about in the boiling water, while the boys, snug and safe in the shelter of the cave, watched the boughs of the pine trees swaying in the wind and waited for Jean to tell them that dinner was ready. She could cook but one thing at a time over the fire, but it was not long before the feast was spread, and they fell to with appetites that caused the food to disappear like dew before the morning sun.

"Losh!" said Sandy, rolling over with his feet to the fire, when he could eat no more, "I thought you said you had a rainy day plan, Chief."

"So I have," said Alan, drawing a little book from his pocket. "I'm going to read to you."

Sandy glanced at the book. "Not poetry, Chief!" he said with alarm. "Surely you don't mean that!"

"It isn't just poetry," said Alan. "It's a story about Roderick Dhu and Clan Alpine, and hunting deer in these very mountains. You'll like it, I know."

Sandy groaned and laid his head on his arm. "Go ahead," he said with resignation. "You're the Chief and I can't help myself."

"I'll be washing up the dishes while you read," said Jean.

"Blaze away," said Jock, who loved books as much as he disliked work.

"It's 'The Lady of the Lake,'" Alan began.

"Oh!" snorted Sandy, to whom Walter Scott was scarcely more than a name, "I thought it was about fighting and robbers, and things like that, and here it's about a lady! and it's about love too, I doubt! I wonder at you, Alan McRae!"

Alan made no reply but began to read. When he reached a line about "Beauty's matchless eye," Sandy snored insultingly and was promptly kicked by Jock. But when Alan reached the lines

"The stag at eve had drunk his fill

Where danced the moon on Monan's rill,"

Sandy sat up and began to think the despised poem might amount to something after all. Jean had finished the dishes by this time and sat cross-legged with her chin in her hand, staring into the fire, as Alan read how the splendid stag pursued by hunters,

"Like crested leader proud and high

Tossed his beamed frontlet to the sky;

A moment gazed adown the dale,

A moment snuffed the tainted gale,"

Then she cried out, "Michty me! It's just exactly like the stag we saw Angus Niel shoot by the tarn; isn't it, now, Alan?"

"And Benvoirlich is the very mountain we can see far away to the south from our house," interrupted Jock, when Alan reached that part of the poem.

"Did the hunters get the stag?" demanded Sandy, and "Go on with the tale," shouted all three. Alan read on and on by the flickering light of the fire, and so absorbed were they all in the story of the region they knew and loved so dearly that a shaft of sunlight from the west shot across the cave, lighting up the gloomy corners, before they realized that the day was far gone and the rain had stopped.

"It's time to go home," said Jean. "The sun is low in the west, and Father and Tam will be coming back wet and hungry from the hills, and no broth hot."

They packed the remainder of their supper carefully away in the basket and left it in the corner of the cave behind the wood-pile, put out every spark of the fire, and picked their way carefully down the wet chasm to the ground.

"Hark," said Jock, as they started home. Faraway in the distance there was the frantic barking of a dog. They stopped and listened.

"It's Tam," said Jean, with conviction, "and he's after something. It's either the rabbit or else he's found a weasel hole," and instantly all the children were off at a bound, tearing through the woods in the direction of the sound. They had been having such a good time they had not once thought of Angus Niel, but as they reached the edge of the forest, there he was, standing behind a tree with his gun pointing toward the little gray house! They stopped short in their wild race and instantly hid themselves among the trees. They could see Tam barking and pawing the ground with the greatest excitement in the open field which lay between the forest and the garden-patch.

"Tam's after the rabbit as sure as sure," Jock whispered to Alan, who had crept with him underneath a spreading pine. "That's the very place where he went after him before. If that old thief kills Tam, I'll—I'll—" Jock could think of no fit punishment for such a crime, and in his rage and excitement would have run right out into the open, after the dog if Alan had not held him by his jacket. "Let go—let go!" said Jock, struggling to get away. "I tell you, if he shoots that dog."

Just then a brown flash appeared from the garden wall, and Tam was after it at a bound, barking like mad. "It's the rabbit, and he's got him—he's got him!" murmured Jock, bouncing up and down with excitement with Alan still clinging to his coat. "Good old dog! good old Tam!" He was watching the dog so intently that he did not see Angus take careful aim, but the moment Tam reached the rabbit, seized it in his teeth, and shook it, a shot rang out; and the dog, with a howl of pain, dropped the rabbit and ran yelping toward the house on three legs, holding the fourth one in the air.

Angus immediately ran out from his hiding-place, leaped the brook, and, dashing up the slope toward the house, picked up the dead rabbit and ran with it back into the woods. The children watched him as he fled, and, the moment he was out of sight, they burst from the shelter of the woods and tore up the hillside to the little gray house.

They found Tam sitting on the doorstep licking his paw and howling. He was instantly surrounded by four amateur doctors all anxious to relieve his pain. Jock ran for water to wash his leg, the flesh of which had been cruelly torn open by the bullet. Jean ransacked the kist for bandages, and Alan held up the injured paw and tried to see if any bones were broken, while Sandy helplessly stroked Tam's tail, murmuring, "Good dog! good old Tam!" as he did so. By dint of their combined efforts the wound was cleansed and carefully bound with a rag, and by the time the Shepherd got home, Tam was lying on the hearth beside the fire, with Alan on his knees before him feeding him broth from a pan.

The Shepherd listened with a darkening brow to the story of Tam's injury. He had heard an account of the stag the day before, so the new revelation of Angus's character did not surprise him, but when Alan rose from his knees and said, "To-morrow the Rob Roy Clan will begin to make Angus Niel wish he'd never been born," Robin Campbell's comment was, "Give him rope enough and he'll hang himself, laddie," and Alan, his black eyes flashing with understanding, answered, "We'll see to it that he gets the rope."

X. ON THE TRAIL

Alan and Sandy left the little gray house in the late afternoon and walked together down the river road toward the village. At the bridge which spanned the stream they parted company, and Alan gave Sandy final instructions as to his duties on the next day. He was to watch Angus Niel's house, which lay some distance north of the village, and see what direction he took as he started upon his daily tour in the forests.

The estate of Glencairn covered a territory so large that Angus could not by any possibility make his rounds in one day or even in one week. The Clan knew well where he had spent his time for the two preceding days, and they thought he would be likely to start in a different direction on the morrow. They did not dare count upon his doing so, however, and so Sandy was detailed to give a positive report as to his movements. The next morning, therefore, found Sandy sitting on a stone dyke not a great way from Angus's house, apparently absorbed in whittling and whistling, but in reality keeping a sharp lookout for any sign of life in the Niel household. He had not long to wait before he saw Angus leave the house and wander away into the forest with his gun on his shoulder. As they had surmised, he took a direction entirely different from his route of the two days before.

Sandy waited until he was out of sight, and then hurried back to the bridge, where he met Alan by appointment, and the two walked briskly on to the little gray house together. When they reached it, the wag-at-the-wall clock was just striking nine, and Jean, her morning work done, was "caning" the hearth with blue chalk as a final touch of elegance to her clean kitchen.

"Come on," said Alan. "I've a plan in my head, and we'll have to start directly if we're going to carry it out. Let me have some of that blue chalk, Jean; we may need it. I've got plenty of food with me, so don't wait to put up anything."

"I'm with you," said Jean, giving a final flourish with the blue chalk before she clapped on her bonnet, and in another minute the Rob Roy Clan was afoot, leaving Tam nursing his wounded paw on the doorstep and gazing after them with pathetic eyes.

They left their luncheon in the cave and hurried on at Alan's command to the little mountain tarn where Angus had killed the stag, and there the Clan gathered about him to hear his plan.

"I've been thinking about this," Alan began, "and I'm sure of two things. Angus must have a place where he puts the game he kills, and he must have somebody to help him. The other man comes along and carries it down the mountain to some point where he can ship it to the city. I say, let's find out where that hiding-place is."

"What will we do with it when we find it?" asked Jean.

"That's where the blue chalk comes in," said Alan. "We'll let him know we've been there!"

"You'll never be writing your name there?" asked Sandy anxiously. "He'd be shooting us next!"

"Oh! Sandy, you're a daft body," said Jean, and Jock added: "Mind the Chief, you dunderhead, and keep your tongue behind your teeth. He's none so addled as you think!"

Sandy subsided a little sulkily, and Alan went on.

"When Angus crossed the lake with the stag he landed right over there by that dead pine tree, for I watched him to see, and the place where he hid the stag can't be far from there, because he came back so soon. We'll just take his boat and see if we can't find it."

"Oh!" gasped Jean, who had never been in a boat in her life, "do you know how to make it go?"

"I can row and I can swim," said Alan, "but I tell you if any one goes bouncing around in the boat, it will be just as bad as being bewitched by the water cow, you'll go to the bottom!"

"I can row, too," said Sandy.

Jean wished she hadn't come, but she was bound she would not show it before the boys, so she said, "Sal! who's afraid?" and when they found the boat, she was the first one in it.

Angus was so sure that no one would find his boat, which was carefully screened by the bushes, that he had not even hidden the oars. So it was soon afloat with Jock at the tiller, Sandy on the bottom, Jean in the prow holding to the sides of the boat, scarcely daring to speak for fear of upsetting it, and Alan at the oars. The lake was smooth, and they reached the opposite shore without mishap, except that twice Alan "caught a crab" and splashed water all over Jock, and Sandy filled both shoes as he jumped out of the boat. They pulled it up under the shelter of the dead pine, anchored it by a stone, and cautiously made their way into the woods.

They were now in a very wild section of the mountains, where it seemed as if no one had ever been since the beginning of the world.

"Just hear the stillness," whispered Jean, keeping close to Jock. There was a sort of trail leading back into the woods, which looked as if it might have been made by wild animals going to the lake for a drink. This they followed for some distance until it became indistinct, and then Alan called the Clan together for counsel.

"We'll go just a little farther," he said, "and then, if we don't see any sign of the place, it may be best to go back, for it is easy to get lost in these woods. We are going east now and luckily the sun is shining. When we do turn back, we must keep the sun behind us and we can't help coming out somewhere on the lake. Remember the pewit call if we lose sight of each other."

They resumed their stealthy walk through the woods, and a few rods farther on came to a wide open space which sloped eastward for some distance down the mountain-side. Here they paused.

"We're getting a good way from the boat," said Jean.

"Yes," said Alan, "and I am just wondering whether we'd better go any farther. We don't want to cross this open space, and I see no sign of Angus's storehouse. I hate to give up, though, for we must be very near it." He searched in every direction with his eyes, and suddenly exclaimed under his breath, "Look there!"

"Where?" breathed the Clan, rigid with excitement.

"Do you see that pile of rocks?" said Alan, pointing into the woods beyond the clearing.

"Yes," said Jock, "but there are rocks all around. I don't see that they're any different from others."

"Maybe not," said Alan, "but I see something that looks like the corner of a hunter's shelter sticking out behind that big boulder, and I say, let's skirt around this open place and see."

"Do you want us all to go?" asked Sandy, hoping the Chief would say no.

"You stay here," Alan answered, to his great relief, "and Jean, you come a little farther with us. Then you and Sandy can keep out of sight and watch. If you see a man, keep still in your places and give the pewit call. Jock and I will go on around the clearing and get a better look at those rocks."

Sandy crouched down in the bracken, and two or three hundred feet farther on Jean stopped also, while Alan and Jock cautiously crept on toward their goal, and, by making a wide detour, approached the rocks from the north instead of the west. As they neared them, it was plain that Alan was right. There really was a shelter built against an overhanging rock and almost concealed from view by pine boughs which formed a screen before it. Little by little the boys crept nearer and nearer, stopping every few steps to be sure there was no sign of life about the place. At last they were within a few feet of the rude camp. The shelter was scarcely more than a hole under the rocks, but there was a blackened spot where there had been a fire, a few pans were standing about, and in one corner a pile of evergreen boughs was covered with well-cured deer-skins. A fresh hide ready to cure was spread out on the rocks near by.

"This is the place," whispered Jock. "There is the skin of the stag. Now what are you going to do?" For answer Alan slipped from behind the rocks, crept stealthily into the camp, and on the underside of the rock wrote in big letters with blue chalk

ANGUS NIEL

POACHER

Your sin has found you out!

R. R. C.

Then he crawled swiftly back out of sight and, followed by Jock, made his way as fast as he could toward Jean's hiding-place. To Jean the time that they were gone seemed hours long. The place was lonely, and she was afraid, not only of their finding the man at home in his wild lodge, but even of brownies and elves.

A rabbit stuck his ears up over a nearby log and scuttled away when he saw her. The leaves made a lonely sound as they rustled over her head, and when at last she saw a black object moving about among the trees at some distance beyond the rock-pile, it is not surprising that she immediately gave the pewit call, loud and clear.

The boys heard it and instantly vanished behind some bushes. The dark object moving among the trees seemed to hear it too and, springing forward, came bounding toward the rocks, barking as it came. Jean was not much less anxious when she knew for certain that it was a dog, for a watch dog in that lonely place might be quite as dangerous as a wolf. Moreover, she soon saw, a little distance behind the dog, a man with a gun on his shoulder. She saw the dog reach the camp and go sniffing about on the rocks, and her heart almost stood still as it gave a deep howl and started away as if it scented game.

"He's on the trail of Alan and Jock," thought Jean, wringing her hands. "Oh, what shall I do? The man will surely follow, for he'll think the dog is after game." She sprang to her feet and ran back to Sandy.

"Come quick," she said in a low voice. "The dog smells them; we must get into the boat and have it ready for the boys to jump into. There is not a moment to lose." She sped past him as she spoke, and Sandy came galloping after.

Alan and Jock, who had seen and heard all that Jean had, were now tearing at top speed through the woods and knew from answering whistles that Jean and Sandy were on the way to the boat.

The man had by this time reached the camp and was staring at the blue chalk-marks on the rock, as if unable to believe his own eyes. He did not stop there long. He saw at once that an enemy had found his hiding-place, and that the dog was on his trail. Leaping down the rocks, he started across the clearing on a run toward the lake, his gun in his hand. Jock and Alan realized that they could hardly reach the landing-place before the dog did, so they changed their course and veered a little to the north, thinking that in this way they stood more chance of concealment and that they could signal the boat and get aboard in a less conspicuous place.

By this dodge the dog lost the scent of the boys and, nosing the ground, found the trail of Sandy and Jean. Baying frightfully he came bounding through the underbrush and arrived at the landing just in time to see Sandy push the boat from the shore with Jean in the bow. Furious at being cheated of his prey, the dog ran back and forth on the shore, making mad leaps in the direction of the boat and barking as if possessed.

"Oh, where are the boys?" cried the distracted Jean. They lingered in an agony of suspense, not daring to leave until they saw that Jock and Alan were safe, and then from a little distance up the shore came the pewit call. Sandy rose to the emergency and, pulling frantically at the oars, succeeded in reaching the point from which the call seemed to come. The scared faces of Jock and Alan rose from the bracken, and in another moment they had leaped into the boat, nearly upsetting it as they did so. Alan seized an oar, and he and Sandy together got the boat out of sight behind a bend in the shore. Here they hid among the bushes on the bank until they saw the man appear at the landing-place, scan the lake carefully, and then go back into the woods, calling the dog to go with him. Even then they were afraid to stir for they did not know whether he had gone back to camp or was stalking about among the trees searching for them.

They waited for what seemed a week but saw nothing further of the man, and when at last they heard the report of a gun and the barking of a dog far away down the mountain, they felt safe. He was evidently looking in another direction for the intruders, and at once Alan gave the word to go back to their own side of the lake. They skirted the shores, keeping a sharp lookout all the while, and at length reached the landing-place. The weary members of the Clan breathed a sigh of relief as they found themselves safe on their own ground again, arid their spirits rose.

Jock told what Alan had written on the rock, and Alan was so much impressed by that achievement that he took out the blue chalk and on a rock by the tarn wrote "Here Angus Niel, gamekeeper and poacher, shot a stag"; and on the stone where the boat had been, he put the mystic initials "R. R. C."

"There," said Alan, pausing to admire his handiwork, "that'll keep him guessing, and scared too."

"What can we do next?"

"Take away his boat," said Jean promptly.

"Good idea!" cried Alan.

"Where can we hide it?" asked Jock.

"I'm mortal hungry," said Sandy. "Couldn't we eat first?"

"No food until this job is done," said the Chief firmly. "We'll never have another chance when we know where the other man and Angus both are. It's now or never!"

"But where shall we hide it?" demanded Jock again.

"I'll tell you," cried Jean, her eyes dancing with mischief. "We can carry it to the burn and float it down to the cave!"

This was a stroke of genius, no less, and every member of the Clan looked upon Jean with respect bordering upon awe. At the point where the lake emptied into the burn there were loose rocks, about which the water rushed in a swift cataract, but, below, the current flowed more gently toward the fall. It was deep only in spots where the trout loved to hide, but it was not a stream anywhere in its course upon which one would launch a boat for pleasure. The rocks were so near the surface that the weight of even one person might ground it, but afloat and empty it might be carried clear to the rocks above the cave. The Clan considered the plan carefully, standing upon the rocky banks.

"How would we guide it?" asked Sandy doubtfully.

"There's a rope on the end of the boat," said Jean promptly, "and we could push it off with sticks if it got stuck."

"Come on," cried Alan, and the four plotters rushed bask to the lake and pulled the boat out of the water. Alan took the prow and Jock took the stern, while Sandy and Jean supported it on each side, and in this way, after many struggles, they succeeded in carrying it to a place below the rapids where they dared launch it.

"I'll hold the rope," said Alan, "and you, Sandy, take an oar and go down the other side of the stream, so you can push it off if it gets stuck on that side."

"How'll I get across?" asked Sandy.

This was a poser at first, but Alan found a way.

"Get into the boat," he said, "and we'll push it across where there aren't any stones sticking up. You can pole it across with your oar, and I'll keep hold of the rope."

Sandy jumped in at once, and the boat, in spite of some swirling, was finally near enough to the opposite bank so he could jump out. This he did, taking the oar with him. It was an exciting journey down stream, for the boat bumped against rocks and caught on fallen trees, and it was a good hour before the children, tired out but triumphant, finally dragged it out of the water just above the falls.

"If we had our rope, we could drag it to the edge of the cliff and let it down in front of the cave," cried Jean in another flash of inspiration, and Sandy instantly rushed down the rock, made the necessary detour, and climbed the secret stair to the cave. He then whistled, and three heads appeared over the top of the cliff.

"I'll throw up the rope and when you let the boat down, I'll steady it," said Sandy.

"Heave away," cried Alan, and after a few trials the rope came flying up on the cliff and was soon looped around the boat. Then the three braced their feet against the rocks and slowly lowered the boat by the rope fastened to the prow, and by their own rope, while Sandy steadied it below. They threw down the rope-end after it, and a few moments later the rapturous Clan hauled the boat into the cave! They sat in it to eat their luncheon and were so lost in admiration of their enterprise and their booty that they did not start home until the level rays of the sun warned them that it was late.

XI. ANGUS NIEL AND THE CANNY CLAN

The days that followed were days of stirring adventure to the Rob Roy Clan, and days of continuous and surprising misery to Angus Niel. Never in his history as gamekeeper of Glen Cairn had he had such experiences. The very trees in the woods seemed to be bewitched. Wherever he went he was followed by some mysterious power that seemed to know his every movement. If he killed any game, the fact was advertised and the place marked by signs in blue chalk. Not only that, but the very path of his approach to the spot was marked by pointing arrows and some such legend as "This way to the glen where Angus Niel killed a deer" would decorate a neighboring rock. On other rocks appeared pertinent questions addressed to him. "How much did you get for the stag?" was one of them, and there were also queries as to where he found the best market for game. He was kept so busy searching the forest for these incriminating signs and rubbing them out, that he could not follow his regular rounds. Even this did not avail, for if he erased them on one day, it was but a matter of time before the letters appeared again as fresh and blue as ever. Nor was this all. He was haunted by a wailing voice which reached him even in the remote fastnesses of the forest. He was sure to hear it if he ventured into the neighborhood of the waterfall, and he usually avoided that region as if it harbored a pestilence.

Once late in the afternoon he shot two hares and hid them under some rocks, intending to carry them across the lake in the morning, but when he went for them, they had disappeared altogether, and above the place where they had been was written in blue chalk, "Sacred to the memory of two hares, killed and hidden here by Angus Niel on June 12th."

When he saw this epitaph, Angus's hair really stood on end with fright, and on the day he found that the boat was gone, leaving no trace, he became absolutely terror-stricken. He sought for it behind every rock and in every likely nook about the lake, consuming days in the quest, and was appalled on his next trip thither to find all the incidents of his search faithfully recorded on the rocks, each one signed with the mystic initials R. R. C.

It took ingenuity, persistence, and some degree of danger on the part of the clan to accomplish these things, but one could depend upon finding these qualities in any Campbell or McGregor, and Sandy, having been made a blood brother, faithfully lived up to the duties it entailed. He became an expert detective and sleuth-hound, discovering and reporting Angus's movements each day to the enterprising Clan and its resourceful Chief.

At Alan's suggestion, the Clan took for its motto "We must be canny," and canny they certainly were. They even changed their programme from day to day, and in this way just when Angus felt he was about to discover his tormentors and know if they were human and not witches, they found some new method of annoyance and he was all at sea again.

Once they gave him a respite of nearly a week and Angus, having erased many signs and finding no new ones, was beginning to think his troubles were over, when suddenly arrows bearing bits of paper inviting him to visit the fall would suddenly drop at his feet. It had taken the Clan nearly all their spare time for the week to make the bows and arrows, by which this wonder was accomplished. Meanwhile they had lived like lords, feasting upon trout and the generous store of provisions with which Alan continued to supply the cave. They even began to see how it was possible for Rob Roy and his men to live upon forest fare, for the pool below the fall was a wonderful fishing-hole, and small game was plentiful if they had cared to become poachers themselves.

On one red-letter day, they roasted the two hares which Angus had killed, and cooked potatoes in the ashes. Each day was filled with fresh adventures, and the wild outdoor life agreed with Alan so well that his thin cheeks began to fill out and glow with healthy color and it was not long before he looked as sturdy and strong as Jock himself.

It was curious that what Alan gained in flesh and spirits, Angus Niel at the same time seemed to lose. He was so worried by these strange visitations that his round eyes took on a haunted expression, and Sandy observed that he kept looking over his shoulder as if he thought some one were following him, even when he walked the village streets.

He dared not stay away from the forest lest others should discover the dreadful blue signs before he did, and at the same time he was afraid to go in. He swung like a pendulum between these two difficulties and grew daily more nervous and unhappy. By the end of June he had lost ten pounds of flesh as well as the money he might have made out of poaching and selling the game. By the middle of July he was so haggard that people began to remark on his appearance. There seemed no way out of his troubles but to lie about them, and soon wild stories were circulated through the village about the haunted forest and its dangers.

Women were warned not to let the children stray into the woods lest they be carried away by witches or water cows, and it was also reported that a gang of poachers of a particularly blood-thirsty character infested the region, carrying off game and property and leaving no trace. Angus had been watching this band of desperadoes for some time, he said, and knew there were at least twenty of them who would stop at nothing.

With Angus's tale of the mysterious loss of his boat, the excitement reached a climax, and there was talk of organizing an armed band of men from the village to protect the woods and rid the neighborhood of the bandits. The people were surprised that Angus himself should oppose this plan, but as he was gamekeeper and in authority, the matter was dropped. To Angus's horror, however, these rumors and events were all faithfully recorded on rocks not far from his own home soon after, and he realized that to the very doors of his own house he was pursued by the same mysterious and vigilant power. It was then that he lost his appetite, and if the Clan could have followed him into his home and seen him look under his bed before he got into it at night, their joy would have been full.

The wild stories he told had the effect of keeping every one else out of the forest and made the Clan more than ever free to stalk their prey without fear of discovery. In this occupation several exciting weeks passed by, and then there came an unhappy surprise to the Clan, and it was not Angus Niel who sprang it upon them either.

One morning in late July, Alan came up the road toward the little gray house, where he was now so much at home, looking very glum indeed.

Sandy was with him, wearing a face as solemn as a funeral procession. Jock and Jean saw them coming and hailed them with a shout, and Tam, who had not quite recovered from his injury, came dashing down the brae on three legs to greet them. Even Tam's joyful bark did not lift the shadow from their faces.

Jean cried out from the top of the brae, "Whatever can be the matter with you? You're looking as miserable as two hens in a rainstorm!"

"Trouble enough," answered Sandy, and Jean and Jock at once came hurrying down the slope to hear the bad news. They met at the river-side, and Sandy, who was bursting to tell it, cried out, "What do you think? Alan's got to go home! His mother's sent for him!" One look at Alan's melancholy face confirmed this dreadful statement and the gloom instantly became general.

The Clan sat down on the ground in a depressed circle to discuss the matter and its bearing on their plans.

"Don't you think your mother would let you stay if you should ask her?" suggested Jock.

"No," said Alan, with sad conviction. "She said I was to come at once, and I'll have to start this very afternoon. I'm to drive down to the boat and get to Glasgow by water; I'll spend the night there and go on to London in the morning."

"Sal, but you'll be seeing a lot of the world," said Jock. "I wish I were going with you."

"I wish you all were," said Alan.

"We'll likely be having more traveling than we want," said Jean, "when we have to give up the wee bit hoosie and go out and walk the world." She looked up at the little gray house as she spoke, and her eyes filled with tears.

"It's the end of the Clan; that's what it is," said Sandy with deepening despondency.

"Oh, come now!" said Alan. "It's not so bad as all that, and I'm surely coming back next summer. I know my mother'll let me, for she'll see how much good it's done me to be here. Just look at that," he added, baring his arm and knotting his biceps. "Climbing around the cave and chasing after Angus Niel have made me as tough as a knot. She won't know me when she sees me."

"I wonder if we shall know you the next time we see you, if we ever do," said Jean.

"Ho!" said Alan, trying to smile gayly, "of course you will! I'll have a sprig of the evergreen pine and give the pewit call, and then you'll be sure."

"What good will your coming back next summer do us?" said Jock. "We shan't be here to see you! Our leases run out in October, and nobody knows where we'll go after that! We've got to move out, so the Auld Laird can have more space to raise game for Angus Niel to kill," he finished bitterly.

There seemed no way of brightening this sad prospect, and the Clan sat for a few moments in mournful silence. Alan tried hard to think of something comforting to say.

"I'll tell you what," he exclaimed at length. "We can still be a Clan, whether we see each other or not. We'll remember we're all blood brothers just the same."

"And that you are our Chief," added Jean, trying to look cheerful.

"Can't we go back to the cave just once more?" said Sandy.

"I've got to be at the bridge at one o'clock," said Alan. "I've said good-bye to Eppie, and she is packing my things, and putting up a lunch, so I don't have to do anything but step into the carriage when I get there. What time is it now?"

Jean flew up the slope to the house and called back from the door, "It's ten o'clock."

"Come on, then, my merry men!" cried Alan, and the four started off at a brisk trot, looking anything but merry as they went.

"We shan't want to come here any more," said Jock, when they reached the cave. "So we may as well take everything away."

"Oh," said Alan, "something might happen to keep you in the Glen Easig. You never can tell. You'd better take back the pots and pans, but leave the wood, and then if we are here next summer, it will be all ready for cooking a jolly old mess of trout."

"Whatever shall we do with the boat?" asked Jean. This was a conundrum, but the Chief, as usual, was equal to the occasion.

"There's only one thing we can do," he said. "It will just dry up and fall to pieces up here; we'll let it down over the rock by the ropes and leave it in the pool. Then when Angus finds it, he'll be perfectly sure he was bewitched and be more afraid of the falls than ever!"

They worked hurriedly, for the time was short, and in another hour the boat was floating in the fishing-pool, securely tied to a pine tree on the bank. They packed pots and pans in the basket and lowered it over the rock by the rope, and when everything was done, Alan took the blue chalk and drew a sprig of pine on the wall of the cave with the initials R. R. C. beside it. The four children then scrambled down the secret stairway, feeling as if they had said good-bye forever to a dear friend. When they reached the little gray house, they left the basket in the kitchen, and the entire Clan walked with Alan back to the bridge, where they found the carriage waiting.

Alan made short work of his good-byes. He shook hands all round and sprang quickly into the carriage, and as it rattled away with him down the road, he stood up, waving his bonnet with the spray of evergreen pine in it and whistling the pewit call.

"Dagon't," said Sandy, when the carriage passed out of sight around a bend in the road. "Dagon't, we'll never find another like the Chief." If Jean and Jock had felt able to say anything, they would have echoed the statement. As it was, Sandy drew his kilmarnock bonnet over his eyes, thrust his hands into his pockets, and started dejectedly toward his own house, leaving Jean and Jock, equally miserable, to return alone to the wee bit hoosie on the brae.

The rest of the week seemed at least a month long to the lonely twins. Sandy came to see them, to be sure, but with the passing of the Chief, the flavor seemed gone from the play, and the Clan made no further expeditions after Angus Niel.

"He can just kill all the game he wants to," said Jean. "It's the worse for the Auld Laird, I doubt, but who cares for that, so long as he leaves Tam alone and keeps away from here? It's nothing to me."

Their father had been so taken up with his work and with turning over in his mind plans for the future, when they should be "walking the world," that he paid little attention to their punishment of Angus Niel, about which he knew little and cared less. He was absorbed in planning the best market for his sheep and in getting as much from his garden as he could, hoping to sell what he was unable to use himself, when the time came to leave. His usually cheerful face had grown more and more troubled as the summer wore on, and it was seldom now that his bagpipes woke the mountain echoes, and whenever he did while away a rainy evening with music, the melodies were as wild and mournful as his own sad thoughts.

Angus Niel's barometer now rose again. Finding himself no longer pursued by his unseen foes, his waning self-confidence returned, and it was only a week or two after Alan's departure that wonderful stories began to go about the village concerning his prowess in ridding the woods of thieves and marauders single-handed.

"I've even found my boat," he announced one evening to a group of men lounging about the village store, "and it was no human hands that put it where I found it either! It was below the falls, if you'll believe me, safe and sound and tight as ever. Any man that is easily scared would better not be walking the woods in that direction, I'm telling you, or likely he'd be whisked away by the little people and shut up in some cave in the hills. I felt the drawing myself once, but I knew how to manage. I was just gey firm with them, and they knew I wasna fearful and let me go. It's none so easy being a gamekeeper. It takes a bold man, and a canny one, and well the poacher gang knew that. They're gone and good riddance. It's taken me all summer to bring it about."

"Oh," murmured Jock to Jean, when this was repeated to them by Sandy the following Sabbath, "wouldn't Alan like to hear that?" It was on that very Sabbath, too, that they learned the Dominie had recovered and that school was to reopen on the following day. This was good news to the Twins, for like all Scotch children they longed for an education, and the next morning, bright and early, they were on the road to the village, carrying some scones and hard-boiled eggs for their luncheon, in a little tin pail.

The days passed swiftly after that, for, with the house to care for, lessons to get, and the walk of five miles to school and back, there was little time for moping or even dreading the day when they must leave their highland home.

It was late August when they came rushing home one afternoon, bursting with a great piece of news, which they had learned in the village. Never had they covered the five miles of the homeward journey more quickly, but when they reached the little gray house, their father had not yet returned from the pastures, though it was after his time. The two children ran back of the house to the cow byre, and there in the distance they saw him coming across the barren moor. He was walking slowly, with his head bent as though he were tired and discouraged, and Tam, limping along beside him, looked discouraged too. The Twins gave a wild whoop and raced across the moor to meet them. Jock got there first, but was too out of breath to speak for an instant.

"Dear, dear! What can the matter be?" said their father, looking from one excited face to the other.

"Oh, Father," gasped Jean, finding her tongue first, "you never can guess, so I'll tell you. The Auld Laird's dead."

The Shepherd stood still in his tracks, too stunned for words.

"Aye!" cried Jock, wishing to share in the glory of such an exciting revelation. "He's as dead as a salt herring."

"Oh, Father!" cried Jean, "aren't you glad? Now we won't have to leave the wee bit hoosie and the Glen."

"I'm none so sure of that," said the Shepherd slowly, when he had recovered from the first shock of surprise. "The new Laird may be worse than the old. Be that as it may, I'm not one to rejoice at the death of any man. Death is a solemn thing, my dawtie, but the Lord's will be done, and I'm not pretending to mourn."

"We went to the village," cried Jean, "to get a bit of meat for the pot, and there was a whole crowd of people around the post-office door. 'T was the post-master gave us the news, and Mr. Craigie and Angus Niel have put weeds on their hats and look as mournful as Tam when he's scolded. We saw them out of the school-house window not two hours gone."

"They have reason to mourn," said the Shepherd grimly, "not for the Auld Laird's death only, but for their own lives as well. Aye, that's a subject for grief." He shook his head dubiously, and, seeming to feel it was an occasion for a moral lesson, he added, "'Mark the perfect man and behold the upright, for the end of that man is peace.'"

"What has that to do with the Auld Laird?" asked Jock, much mystified.

"Nothing at all, maybe," answered the Shepherd, "but it's a wise word to remember against our own time."

"I wish Angus Niel would remember it," exclaimed Jean.

"And Mr. Craigie no less," added Jock.

"Well, well," said the Shepherd, "heard ye anything more in the village?"

"Aye, that we did," said Jean, who loved to prolong the excitement of news.

"Let me tell that," said Jock. "You told about the Auld Laird. Well, then, Father, there's all kinds of tales about the new Laird. It's said he's a wee bit of a laddie, not more than four years old, and not the son of the Auld Laird at all, but a cousin or something. It's said he's weak and sickly-like and not long for this world."

"Sandy's mother was in the village and walked with us to the bridge," interrupted Jean, "and she heard that the heir is a young man living in

Edinburgh, and not even known to the Auld Laird, who had no near kin. She had it from the minister's wife, so it must be true."

"Didn't Mr. Craigie say anything? He ought to know more about it than any one. He's the Auld Laird's factor to carry out his will while he was living. It's likely he'd know more than any other about his will, now he's dead," said the Shepherd.

"Mrs. Crumpet says he goes about with his mouth shut up as tight as an egg, as though he knew a great deal more than other folk, being so intimate-like with the Laird," said Jean.

"Aye!" added Jock, "but she said she believed there was a muckle he did not know at all, and he was keeping his mouth shut to make folks think he knew but wasna telling."

Jean now took up the tale. "Mrs. Crumpet had all the news in town," she said, "and she told us that Angus Niel said he hoped the new Laird was fond of the hunting and would appreciate his work in preserving the game and driving poachers from the forests of Glen Cairn. He said he had done the work of ten men, and it was well that people should know it and be able to tell the new Laird, when he comes into his own!"

Even the Shepherd couldn't help smiling at that, and as for Jean and Jock, they shouted with laughter. In spite of themselves, the children and their father felt such relief from anxiety that they walked back to the little gray house with lighter hearts than they had felt for some time. Whoever the new Laird might be, it would take time to settle the estate and find out the will of its new owner, and meanwhile they could live on in their old home. Beyond that, they could even hope that they might not have to go at all.

That night Jean cooked the first of their early potatoes from the garden for supper and a bit of ham to eat with them, by way of celebrating their reprieve, and after supper the Shepherd got out his bagpipes and played "The Blue Bells of Scotland" until the rafters rang again. Jean stepped busily about the kitchen in tune to the music, humming the words to herself.

"Oh where, tell me where is your Highland laddie gone?

He's gone with streaming banners where noble deeds are done,

And it's oh! in my heart, I wish him safe at home."

And she thought of Alan as she sang. Afterward, when Jock and Jean were safely stowed away for the night, the Shepherd went over and brought from the table in the room his well-worn copy of Robert Burns's "Poems," and the last view Jean had of him before she went to sleep, he was reading "The Cotter's Saturday Night" aloud to himself by the light of a flickering candle.

XIII. THE NEW LAIRD

It was Friday when news of the Auld Laird's death reached the village, and on the following Sabbath there was not an empty seat in the kirk, for every one was anxious to hear the latest gossip about the event which meant so much to every one in the region. There was no newspaper in the village, and the news of the week was passed about by word of mouth in the kirkyard after service, or on week days was retailed over the counter at the village post-office, which was post-office and general store in one.

The Campbells were early in their pew, and the Twins watched the other worshipers as they came slowly up the aisle and took their places before time for the service to begin. Sandy winked at them most indecorously across the church, but his mother poked him to remind him of his duty, and he sent no more silent messages to the other members of the Clan.

There was an air of expectation, which seemed to affect every one in the kirk. Even the minister looked as if he had something special on his mind, and as for Mr. Craigie, he was as solemnly important, Sandy said afterwards, "as though he were the corpse himself," while Angus Niel acted like nothing less than the chief mourner.

In the kirkyard he let it be known that he was entirely familiar with the details of the Auld Laird's funeral, which had occurred in London the day before, though how the particulars reached him in so short a time must forever remain a mystery.

It was Mr. Craigie, however, who gave out the important news which every one had felt must be coming. On the steps after service he said to Mr. Crumpet, "It's likely, Andrew, that you may have more time about your lease. I've had news that the new Laird is coming soon to the castle with his lawyers and some other people to look over the estate and take possession. Eppie McLean is to get ready for quite a party of the gentry."

Mrs. Crumpet was standing near her husband, and she was a bold woman who would have asked a question of the Auld Laird himself, if she had had occasion. "Then it's the sickly bit laddie who's the heir?" she said, "and not the Edinburgh man?"

Mr. Craigie looked majestic and waved her aside, merely saying, as he went down the steps, "It isna an Edinburgh body," but giving no hint as to whether it was man, woman, or child. The people who had gathered about him thinking to hear something definite looked resentfully at his back as he walked away, and Mrs. Crumpet openly expressed her opinion that he knew nothing more about it himself. "If he did, he couldn't help letting it dribble out by degrees, like a leaky kirn, being too stingy to tell it out free, like any other body," she said.

Mrs. Crumpet was a woman of rare penetration. Even Sandy didn't often get ahead of his mother.

For another week the village waited in suspense for further news, and then on Saturday the report spread like wildfire through the town that the new Laird with his party had arrived at the castle the night before.

It was Sandy who brought the news to the little gray house. "And they say there were three carriage-loads of them and they never got to Glen Cairn until dark," he cried; "and the tale is that the castle ovens have never been cool since the word came a week ago! Mother says Eppie McLean has been laying in provisions as if she looked for seven lean years like Joseph in Egypt."

"Losh!" interrupted Jock, "I wish Alan was here. Wouldn't we get some of those good things for the cave, though."

"But that isn't all the news," cried Sandy, who had come three miles to tell it and was not going to let it burst from him too suddenly. "There's more."

"What is it, Sandy?" cried Jean, dancing with impatience. "Hurry, lad; let out what's bottled up in you or you'll blow the cork!"

"Well," exploded Sandy, "you'll get some of the good things without Alan, I'm telling you, for there's to be a grand feast at the castle, and everybody is asked to come! There's a sign up in the village, and it's to be Monday at five o'clock. They say Eppie McLean has fowls waiting by the dozen and a barrel of tatties ready for the pot. Losh! I don't see how the new Laird can stay weakly with so much to fill him up."

"Sal!" cried Jean, "if he's such a wee laddie as they say, it's likely his mother will be the one to say what's to be done in Glen Cairn, and it's not likely she'll be wanting to go rampaging over the country shooting game like the Auld Laird."

"Ye can never tell," said Sandy, with a worldly air. "Some say ladies is worse than men."

"Never believe that," said Jean, promptly, and then she added a little wistfully, "especially if they are mothers."

At church the next day the congregation was in such a state of excitement it was with the greatest difficulty that the proper Sabbath decorum was observed. Sandy Crumpet brazenly looked over his shoulder every time any one passed up the aisle, thinking that perhaps the new Laird and his mother might come in at any moment, and even the grown people looked sidewise, but no new faces appeared and fear was expressed afterwards that the mother of the heir was of the Established Church. Mrs. Crumpet said she had always heard that among the gentry the women were fiercer in their religion than the men. The Shepherd remembered the Laird of Kinross, but said nothing.

On the way home from church Jean and Jock noticed that smoke was issuing from all the castle chimneys. It was now early autumn, and, as Jean said, the castle must be damp from, standing so long empty, and they had the right to warm it up for the wee Laird, him being so sickly.

The suspense of the long weeks of summer had now become acute. If the Auld Laird's wish to turn the tenants out of their holdings to make Glen Cairn into a large game preserve was to be carried out, the time for doing it was near, and the people looked forward to the supper at the castle with both hope and dread.

Every one was to be there, and on Monday a wonderful amount of preparation was going forward in every cottage and farmhouse on the estate. Jean had her father's blacks on the line and thoroughly brushed early in the morning, and the Sabbath clothes for all three of them laid out on the chairs in "the room" by noon. At four o'clock they were on their way to the castle. Jock had wanted to start at three, but Jean was firm.

"It isna genteel to be going so early," she said. "T'will look greedy, and you'll not get fed the sooner."

Any one would have said Jean looked pretty that day, for she was not wearing her "Saturday face," and the little curls had crept around her head unbeknownst and were blowing in bright tendrils about her forehead under the edge of her bonnet with its sprig of pine. Her cheeks were pink and her eyes bright with health and excitement, and Robert Campbell, looking with pride at his sturdy son and daughter, said to himself, "It's a sonsie lassie and braw lad. I wish their mother could see them."

They walked down the river road, where the autumn colors were beginning to appear, and at the bridge met the Crumpet family all dressed in their best, also on their way to the castle. Sandy had scrubbed himself till his face was shining like a glass bottle, and the sprig of pine waved proudly from his bonnet, too. At every branch road they were joined by others, and when they neared the castle gates there was already quite a large group of people from the village as well. Every one was in a state of tense excitement, for the fate of all hung in the balance. Since the tenure of their homes was at the mercy of the new Laird, his ideas and disposition were of vital importance in their lives, and they were keen to see him and find out for themselves what manner of person he might be. Mr. Crumpet was looking very glum. He took a morose view of life at best, and the present circumstances certainly warranted apprehension.

"If it's a wee bit of a laddie, as we are led to expect," he said to the Shepherd, "he'll have no judgment of his own, and be dependent on them as has him in charge. Mr. Craigie will not be loosening his hold, and with only a weak woman and a sickly boy to deal with, he'll wind 'em around his finger like a wisp o' wool. It's my opinion we'll have Mr. Craigie to deal with more than ever."

"Well," said Mrs. Crumpet philosophically, "and if we jump at all 't will be but from the fire back to the frying-pan again, I'm thinking."

Various other opinions were expressed by one and another as the tenants of Glen Cairn followed the wide drive which led to the castle doors. Most of them had never before been inside the walls of the park, and they looked about them with interest at the unkempt and overgrown drive and at the bracken and heather spreading even over the lawns. It was evident that the place had been left to take care of itself for many years.

It was a warm day in late September, and though there was a touch of red in the ivy which draped the gray castle walls, the air was mellow with the haze of autumn and musical with the buzzing of bees.

Mr. Craigie, looking more like a pair of tongs than ever, stood on the terrace with the minister and his wife, while Angus Niel, swelling with importance, ranged round the outskirts of the crowd as they approached the castle, gradually herding them toward the entrance. When they were all gathered in front of the terrace, the minister came forward to the steps and lifted his hand. A hush instantly fell upon the waiting people, and the minister spoke.

"Her ladyship has asked me to say to you that she and the new Laird will meet you here," he said, "and afterward conduct you to the banqueting-hall, where supper will be served. It is their desire to know you all personally, and I will be here to present you as you come up the steps."

There was a surprised look on every face as the minister finished speaking. What manner of landlord could this be, who made a point of knowing his tenants as men and women the moment he came to the estate? It was a breathless moment when at last the great castle doors swung open, revealing a group of people standing in the entrance. There was an instant's pause, and then a tall strong-looking woman stepped forward upon the terrace, with her hand resting lightly on the shoulder of a sturdy black-haired boy nearly as tall as herself. The boy was dressed in kilts, with the Campbell plaid flung over his shoulder and a spray of evergreen pine nodding gayly from his Glengarry bonnet.

"Michty me! It's Alan!" exclaimed Jock, so stunned by surprise that his knees nearly gave way under him, while Jean, her eyes shining like stars, clutched her father's hand, too stunned to realize at first that Alan and the new Laird of Glen Cairn were one and the same person. In fact, nobody realized it at once, for many of the tenants had come to know and like Alan during the summer, simply as "the boy who was staying with Eppie McLean."

They were still gazing at the castle door and wondering why the "puny wee laddie, who was not long for this world" did not appear, when the gracious lady, who still stood with her hand resting proudly on Alan's shoulder, began to speak.

"Many of you already know the new Laird of Glen Cairn as Alan McCrae," she said, smiling kindly down into their blank upturned faces. "He has been among you all summer and has learned to love our Highland country without dreaming that he himself would one day inherit this beautiful estate. He is next of kin to the Auld Laird, though not a near relative, and had no idea that I had any purpose beyond the improvement of his health in sending him here for the summer. I knew that which he did not, that he was likely soon to be called to take the Auld Laird's place here, and I wanted him to know you first, not as tenants, but as friends merely. He has come to love this region for its own sake, and comes among you like a true Scotchman, meaning to make this his home and the interests of this community his own interests. He is not yet of age, as you see, but his purposes and plans are clearly formed, and I will leave him to explain them to you himself."

She stopped speaking, and the people, overwhelmed with surprise and joy, burst into a hearty and prolonged cheer, as Alan stepped forward to make his speech. He was only a boy, and a very much embarrassed one at that, but he knew what he wanted to say and he got to the point at once.

"I just want you to know," he said, "that nobody's going to be turned out if he doesn't want to be. I know all about the lease, and that it's going to run out this fall, but any one who wants to stay on the land and improve it is going to have the chance to do it. My mother knows a lot about such things, and we're going to collect the rents ourselves, and we think, maybe, when I'm of age, there'll be some way by which people who really want to use the land may own it instead of being obliged to rent. Mother says they are beginning to do it in Ireland, and in England too in some places.

"I've found out that people are more important than rabbits and deer, and they are going to have first chance at the land of Glen Cairn as long as I'm Laird." This was greeted with such a roar of cheers that for a moment it was quite impossible for Alan to proceed. He smiled bashfully at his mother and then held up his hand for silence.

"I just want to say, too," he went on, biting his lips to keep from laughing, "that after this there won't be any gamekeeper on Glen Cairn. If the rabbits spoil your crops you're welcome to catch them if you can! I've ranged these woods myself all summer, and I have found out that gamekeepers are no safeguard against poachers." A gasp of astonishment greeted this statement, and Angus Niel was observed to turn ashy pale.

"In fact, I know that sometimes gamekeepers turn poachers themselves and make money selling what they have killed," he went on. Here Angus Niel, looking suddenly deflated, like a burst balloon, began quietly to slink out of sight, and Alan, brimful of mischief, raised his voice so it would be sure to reach him and said, "I've seen it done myself, and if Angus Niel wants to know any more about that gang of twenty blood-thirsty villains which has scared the life out of him all summer, he can come to me and I'll tell him. I'm the Chief of that gang, and there are three others just like me, and that's all!" He winked rapturously at the three other members of the Clan, who were gazing up at him in a stupor of astonishment, and fired his last shot at the fleeing Angus, while the audience, catching his meaning, burst into howls of derisive laughter.

"Don't hurry, Angus," he called. "I want to tell you about your boat and about the water witch that haunted you. I'm the water witch too!" But Angus was already out of hearing and scuttling as fast as his trembling legs could carry him to get out of sight, as well. When the roars of laughter had subsided, Alan said, with a boyish grin, "It's too bad he couldn't stay to supper. And now come up, everybody, and meet my mother."

It was then that the Shepherd of Glen Easig astonished himself and every one else by shouting at the top of his lungs, "Three cheers for the young Laird!" and when they had been given with such energy that the hills rang with the echoes, he called for three more for her ladyship, and Alan waved his cap in acknowledgment for them both.

Then the people, surprised out of their usual Scotch reserve by laughter and by the joy of good news, came swarming up the steps and were introduced to Alan's mother by Alan himself when he knew them, and by the minister when he did not.

The Shepherd, with the bashful Clan in his wake, came last of all, and the Twins heard him say to her ladyship, "God bless the laddie! It was a rare day for the Glen when he fell into the burn and came to dry himself by our fireside."

"It was a rare day for me, too, Cousin Campbell," said Alan, and then; catching sight of Sandy and the Twins hanging back behind their father, what did he do but pucker up his lips and whistle the pewit call? The Clan was too overcome then even to attempt a pucker, and Alan, springing forward, tried to grasp three hands at once and introduced them to his mother as his Rob Roy Clan.

The Twins and Sandy were not a bit like the bold buccaneers of the cave when the great lady of Glen Cairn smiled on them kindly.

"I told you I'd wear the sprig of evergreen pine and whistle the call of the Clan the next time you saw me," cried Alan, as they fell in behind the others, who were now entering the banquet-hall. "Why didn't you answer?"

"Oh, but," said Jean, a little sadly and blushing like a poppy, "we never thought you'd be coming back so grand like. You'll never be playing with the Clan any more in Glen Easig, surely, now that you 're a great Laird!"

"And why not, I'd like to know?" cried the great Laird, looking hurt. "I'm still Alan McRae, Chief of the Clan, the same as before, and as true to my friends as Rob Roy himself was before me. We'll have many a good day in the woods yet before snow flies; and listen, I've a plan in my head!"

"There speaks the Chief," cried Jock, forgetting to be afraid of him. "He was ever having plans in his head. Out with it, man."

"It's this," said Alan, "I'm going to have a tutor here at the castle, and you're all to have your lessons here with me, and no end of larks!" Here Sandy, who had so far merely gazed at his Chief with speechless devotion, suddenly burst into words.

"Aye, Chief," he cried, "that was a true word you spoke about no gamekeeper being needed in Glen Cairn. I'm none so keen for the learning, but if there should be poachers hanging about, they'll have Sandy Crumpet to deal with; let them take warning of that!"

Alan laughed and clapped Sandy on the back. "I'd rather have you than forty Angus Niels," he said, and then they were swept along, without a chance for further words, into the great hall, where they found long tables spread and Eppie McLean with a dozen helpers bringing in such stores of food that all Sandy had said about the preparations at the castle was justified at a glance.

Most of the people had already found places at the tables when the young Laird and his mother, followed by the minister and his wife and the castle guests, cams into the hall. The Twins and Sandy hung back behind all the other guests, but Alan found places for them opposite his own, and then he handed his mother to the seat of honor at the head of the table. The minister and the guests from the city ranged themselves on either side, and every one stood with bowed head while the minister asked a blessing upon the food, upon the new Laird and his mother, and upon all the people of Glen Cairn.

There was a great scraping of chairs, and then every one sat down and fell upon the good things like an army of locusts upon a harvest field. The great hall, so long silent, echoed with happy voices and the clatter, of knives and forks, and Jean, looking across the table at the new Laird, in all his glory, wondered if it could be possible that it was the very Alan whom she had shaken when Angus shot the stag, or who had helped her set the table in the kitchen of the little gray house, while his wet clothes were drying by the cottage fire. She ate her supper like one in a dream, and though she kept a watchful eye on Jock's table manners and warned Sandy's elbows off the table several times in her own efficient way, she could scarcely believe such wonderful things were really happening to her.

At last the wonderful day drew to a close, and the people of Glen Cairn, happier than they had been in a long time, said good-bye to the gracious lady of the castle and to the already beloved young Laird, and started home in the deepening twilight of the autumn evening.

The Clan, lingering behind their parents, looked back at the group on the castle terrace before the trees hid them from sight, and Jock sent the pewit call shrilling through the dusk. It was answered instantly from the terrace.

"He is just like Prince Charlie, I'm thinking," said Sandy, and Jock, to ease his feelings, whistled "Charlie is my darling" all the way to the gate of the park.

The evening star was shining brightly over the dark outline of old Ben Vane as the Campbells reached the little gray house on the brae, now safely their home forever, and Tam came bounding down the path to meet them. Jean kissed her hand to the star and murmured to herself,

"Star light, star bright,

I have the wish I wished to-night."